A KINGDOM OF COURAGE AND CRUELTY

BOOK 3

THE LEVANTHRIA SERIES

A.P BESWICK

ISBN - 978-1-7398218-7-6

Editing by Quill & Bone Editing

Cover Art by - Rafido Designs

Proof Read - Alexandrea Sward

❀ Created with Vellum

LEGENDS OF LEVANTHRIA

To The Legends Of Levanthria who have supported each of
the books in the series so far on Kickstarter.
Thank you

The Merry Men.... And Women
Seth (The Little) Alexander
Joshua (The Scarlett) Gray
Daniel (The Friar) Dorman
Robin (The Hood) Hill

The Legendary Pieces Of Eight
Seth (Blackbeard) Alexander
Z (The Sparrow)

LEGENDS OF LEVANTHRIA

The Fallen

J. Garrett
Vanessa Montejano Johnston
Priska
Michael Harrin
Ben Trotter

LEGENDS OF LEVANTHRIA

The Dragon

Louis Jay Dombroski
Jen Smith
Zaakir (The Archer) Patel
Sunny Side Up
Señor Neo
Jacob Salm
Rhonda K Koenning
Brandon H Beers
Jeremiah Silva
Seth Alexander
Christopher Simard
Matthew Schaaff
Armin Enjoyer of Well Written Books
Damien Troutman
Meredith Carstens
Tanya Hagel
Michael William Alexander Gonser

LEGENDS OF LEVANTHRIA

The Dragon

Andrew Sheridan
Ian White
Geoff Seutter
R. S. Howell
Brian R Knoblich
Kevin Camps
Benjamin Powell
Oliver Stegmann
Lauren O'Connor
Travis Hawkins
Joshua Gray
Troy Hauck, RN
Kat Holder
Christian Mays
Dominic Jones
Charlotte Lotte de Reuver
Valerie Wiechmann and Shane Libihoul

Levanthria

erian Plains

Uster

ntar

Yugo's Tears

N

Rivah

Voraz

Zakron Keep

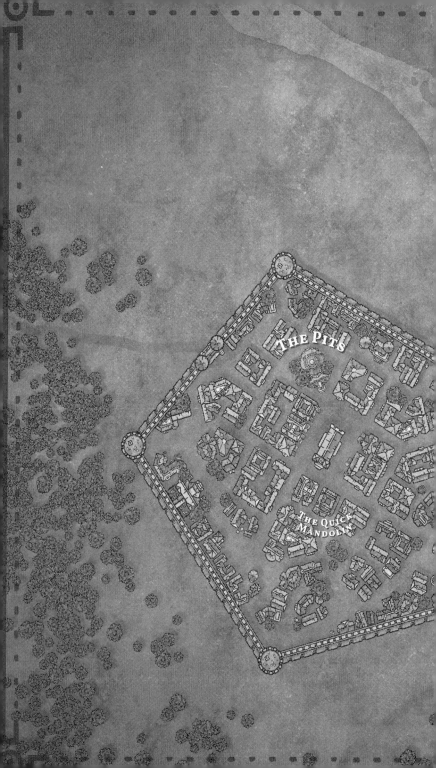

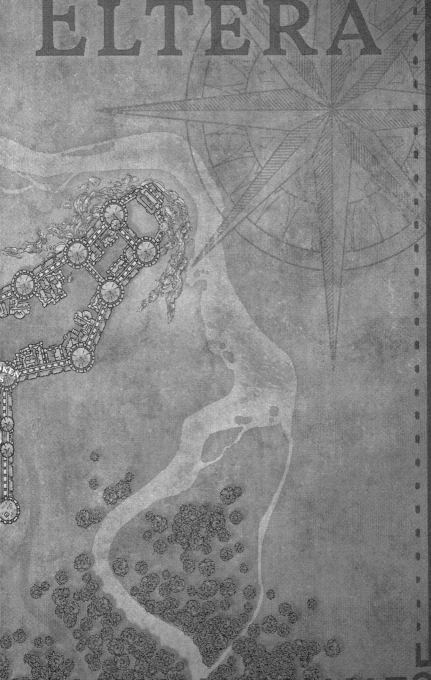

ELTERA

A KINGDOM OF COURAGE AND CRUELTY

PROLOGUE - MORGANA

Freshly cooked bread has never smelt so good. The fragrance sends my ravenous stomach into overdrive, the growl of which is so loud, I fear it may draw attention to me. With full access to the castle, I don't have to sneak around, but at least this way I can hone my powers whilst also having a bit of fun.

Tilting my head up, I allow the luxurious smell to engulf my nose once more before scurrying across the cold stone floor. My nails catch against the surface as I cover ground quickly. The pads on my feet tingle with an icy sting as if I walk in snow, but the sensation helps keep me grounded, focused. Above me, steam rises from the table; I've found the bread. My stomach gives another grumble, this time causing my muscles to gripe. When the cook leaves to gather some ingredients, I seize my opportunity. I rush at the legs of the table and use my nails to cling to the wood as I ascend to the tabletop. My eyes widen at the sight of the crisp, warm bread in front of me. The warmth it emits brings me comfort as if I sit in front of a fire. I waste no time tearing into it, not even caring when the heat stings my mouth. I wildly devour the side of the loaf, oblivious to my surroundings.

"Fucking rats!"

The voice of the agitated chef startles my attention, and as I look up at the giant's frame, it is already too late. In his right hand he grasps a rolling pin which he brings down on me with incredible force.

In an instant, my connection to the rodent is severed and I find myself sitting in front of my intricately carved vanity table. In the reflection, my emerald-green, bloodshot eyes stare back at me, and sweat beads on my forehead from the strain of using my magic. Possession is a method I have been honing for a while now. Like other spells, the more I practice, the stronger I become, and the longer I can maintain the connection.

I allow myself a few moments to reacclimatise to my own body, quickly taking a sip of water to quell the familiar urge to vomit. I take out my journal from the drawer to my right and add my new findings to my notes.

"Connection severed when possessed body's life is ended," I speak as I write the words, coughing to clear my throat in the process. I had become reckless, engrossed in the moment as I let my acquired rat senses distract me. I am grateful that the chef's actions merely severed our connection; up until now, I had never experienced something like that.

After I finish my notes and lock my journal away, I return my gaze to the mirror and search over the woman that sits before me. The glint of my necklace catches the candlelight. I bring my hand to hold the charm that sits at the nape of my neck, closing my eyes.

My temporary moment of solace is interrupted by a

brisk, sudden knock at the door. It jolts my eyes open and my nostrils flare with frustration.

"What is it?" I ask curtly.

"It's a letter," a nervous voice calls back.

"I am not dressed. Leave it by the door and I will read it when I am ready." The unwelcome distraction sours my mood.

"I'm sorry, my lady," the voice stammers, "it's just, the letter has the king's seal on it."

Now that does capture my attention. I push my chair back quickly, the legs squeaking against the stone floor.

"Come in," I call out.

The door creaks as it is heaved open by one of the guards, and a young man approaches me with the letter in his hand. Trembling, the man passes it to me as quickly as possible. King Athos Almerion's seal is fixed to one side of the envelope: three swords pointing down with a third pointing upwards through the middle.

"That is all." I cast my eyes to the guard who shuffles his tunic straight before exiting, closing the door behind him. He leaves me to my own comfort once more. Just as I like it.

I remove the letter from its envelope and pore over the king's words:

Morgana,

I have received a report regarding the condition of Eltera following the witch trials. It causes me great concern to learn that after three years, Lord Wistler is unable to bring order about the people to ensure taxes are collected in a timely manner. With my forces stretched thin, we need all available resources if we are to finally end this war and claim these lands as our own. The spell-casters you trained have proven most helpful, but as you warned, their continued magic use takes a toll on their bodies, rendering them useless. For this reason, I request that you continue your experiments around magic and continue to train those that are able to wield magic so that they can aid us."

I do have one further request of you. If you can fulfil it, it will certainly put you in my favour when I return. As Codrin currently stands as ward over Askela, I need you to go to Eltera. I need you to find out why Lord Wistler is unable to get control of his people and ensure that coin and weapons are being provided for our forces. Their forge is renowned for producing the strongest armour in Levanthria and it is imperative that we regain use of it. Head to Eltera, take back control, and help me end this war against the Zarubians. Because Eltera is the nearest city to the southern ports, I fear that foreign forces such as the Barbaraqs may seek to take advantage of my absence. Eltera cannot fall. Levanthria's fate may depend upon it.

I will make this more than worth your while when I return. After all, a king needs a queen.

Kindest regards,

King Athos Almerion

My chest pulses as I finish reading the letter. Did I read right? Is King Athos offering to make me his queen if I am successful? I would need to postpone my experiments if I were to make for Eltera.

"Guards," I call out, and the door creaks open once more. "Have a carriage prepared for me. It would appear that the king has a request of me in Eltera."

"Right away, Lady Morgana," the nervous guard responds, a quake in his voice. "Your maids have arrived with your breakfast."

When my maids enter, one opens the doors to my wardrobe and starts to prepare my clothes for the day.

The younger one slides me a tray laden with fruit and bread. "Morning, Lady Morgana," she says.

My eyes widen and my nostrils flare when I see the

bread that has been presented to me. It is the fresh bread that I have already sampled whilst in possession of the rat.

"Guards!" I shriek. "Have the cook brought to me at once." I will not have it that he knowingly served me food tainted by rats – an insolence I will make him pay for before I leave.

1

ORJAN

"*Ironite ore is a rare mineral only found deep within the caves of Drangor. These ancient mines sit outside of Levanthria but under King Athos Almerion's reign the kingdom has remained in control of the mines.*"
Jonah Viergen, Minerals and Ore's of the lands, 260KR

RAUCOUS LAUGHTER FILLS THE TAVERN, the merrymakers clinking their tankards together vigorously, sloshing ale all over the place. Two men barely notice me as one of them knocks into my shoulder, but I hold my tongue; I do not wish to draw attention to myself. A thick musk fills the air, a musk that brings me comfort but also fills me with regret.

To my left, a group of solemn hunters talk about their day's work, their faces downcast with only but a few rabbits lined up on the ale-soaked table. Wolf pelts that have seen better days adorn their shoulders. To my right, an older man is in deep conversation with scantily clad men and women of the night, their clothing leaving little to the imagination as they pour drinks to ease the task of negotiating their services.

I drink to forget. I drink to numb my memories, to make it all go away. No one bothers me, but I draw curious stares because of my size. I tend to keep out of anyone's business. That is, unless they make it my business.

I sit in the corner with my cloak drawn over my hideously disfigured face. I am a repulsion, which is no more than I deserve for my past sins. But I find it ironic that this curse befell me whilst trying to do the right thing for once. How the gods tease me. If I had the power, I would strike them all down with vengeance.

I unfurl a scaled hand around my tankard and drink, searching for the bottom. All I find is misery.

Taking note of a few men eyeing me up, I know it's time to take my leave. I slam three coins on the bar before taking the bottle of whiskey that sits there. I head for the door, each staggered step laboured and drawn. The curse I carry not only disfigured my appearance, but it also has changed how drink affects me. I push my way outside, hunching my back so as not to reveal my true height. Once the door closes behind me, the laughing and joking becomes mumbled and distant.

Muck and water splash up my legs as I stumble my way up the street, failing miserably at dodging the puddles of horseshit that pool between the broken cobblestones. The sound of the wind picking up is a sign that it's going to be a stormy night, but my thick hide protects me from the cold that darkness brings. Neither cold nor warmth can penetrate the scales that decorate my cursed body. My tolerance of the seasons is much higher than it once was.

Taking a large gulp of whiskey as I walk, I savour the

warmth that follows the sweetness of the bourbon in the back of my throat, leading down into my insides. At least I can still feel that.

Trudging through the pooling mud, I make to find some shelter where I can settle for the night. The toxins from the whiskey begin to take effect, and the blurred flames of streetlamps flicker as I make my way to the shelter I spotted earlier today. I have found that in this form, whiskey affects me the most, even if I like its taste the least.

Mud splashes behind me. I stumble to a stop and search over my shoulder to see what the night has brought me this time.

"Give us your coin," the man demands. The whiskey merges his features together and I can't make out his face. Two other darkened figures stand to either side of him.

"I said, give us your coin." He brings his arm forward, revealing a small blade.

I laugh to myself and turn away from my would-be muggers, continuing my walk down the street. They are not the first to try and rob me in the dead of the night, and I think I can safely say they will not be the last.

"Something wrong with your ears?" the man calls after me, his voice whiney and irritating.

I flick my hand to wave them away. All I want is to find the bridge I seek and drink my whiskey until I pass out.

"I said, give me your coin!"

"Leave." My voice is deep, threatening. "Whilst you can."

The men snigger in response.

I take in a large breath and stand up straight, revealing my true height, my fake hunch no more. They saw me as a feeble, drunken man. How they were wrong. How they were so wrong. Turning to face them, I lower the cloth covering my face, letting them see my yellow eyes, my pointed features, my scaled skin.

The men stare at me, speechless. I do not know if this is in disbelief or fear, and I do not care. I am in no mood for a fight.

"It's him," one of them speaks.

"I've heard stories of him. He – he's a –"

"A beast? A monster?" I emit a low growl as I speak. "A creature of the shadows. Lizard man. The monster of Mahrua?" I start quoting the different names I've heard on my travels.

"You . . . you . . ." the man with the knife stutters, unable to form his words. "You're a . . ."

"Dragon?" I finish his sentence with a snarl as I step into the small plume of the nearest light, making sure they can see my every feature. I have tried everything to rid myself of this curse, to no avail. I may as well use it to my advantage when I need to.

"We mean you no harm," one man says quickly. The three of them turn and scutter down the streets like rats escaping a flood. They are cowards. They know not of honour. If only they knew who I was, if only they knew the things I have seen. The things I have done.

A cursed knight, fallen from grace, plagued by my hideous appearance. As the men leave me, I step back into the shadows, raising the bottle of whiskey to take another large drink.

This is my life now. It has been for years, the other side of my curse. I wander the land, never settling anywhere. People fear me, villages will not accept me. If I stay anywhere too long, it is always only a matter of time before the people take up arms and drive me out.

When I reach the shelter beneath the bridge, I lose my footing, falling backwards into the mud. I let out a heavy sigh and raise my bottle of whiskey, my breath kissing the cold air. I will drink this until I pass out. It is the only way I sleep, it is the only way that I find solitude.

2

MORGANA

The crow's cries wake me. Darkness still surrounds me beyond the last embers in the hearth at the foot of my chambers. This is the third time in as many days that I have been woken in the dead of night from disturbing dreams – all of them as vicious and bloody as the Great War, all of them resulting in my death.

I sit up, letting out a restless huff of air. The chef's young apprentice lies naked beside me, peaceful in his slumber. What I wouldn't give to sleep so serenely, but each time I close my eyes to rest, I see my demise, I see my death.

In my dreams, I'm standing on the crumbling walls of Zakron's Keep to the southeast of Askela. The ruins have not housed a king or queen for millennia, but my visions show this castle being brought back from ruin to its former glory.

It is here where I see my death, where I see a fierce battle at the top of the western tower. One that pits me against that boy, Laith. Except in my dreams he is no longer a boy, but a man. A man with hatred in his eyes, one with a disgust so deep rooted that I know in my final moments I must have wronged him somehow.

It has been three years since I last laid eyes on Laith, tied to a post and broken. Codrin had stripped Laith's skin from bone before he was rescued by Jordell, escaping into the deep Forest of Opiya.

Askela has had prolonged troubles at the hands of that rogue, Vireo. My spies keep me updated on his endeavours whilst I travel Levanthria searching for a way to increase my power.

Despite Vireo proving to be a constant thorn in my side all these years, I have heard nothing of Laith or Jordell. They simply vanished into the mists like spectres. As long as I don't know their whereabouts, I am sure I will continue to have these nightmarish visions. Until Laith is dead, I will not be at peace.

I pour myself some water from a tankard that sits on a chest of ornate drawers at the far side of the room. The cold metal is refreshing against my warm skin, and the cold water, which is flavoured with a slice of haruga fruit, refreshes my dry throat, bringing an enjoyable bittersweet aftertaste.

Because of that blasted boy, I can't find peace, even in the dead of night. His sword buries deep into my stomach as he pulls in close and whispers something in my ear. I do not know what words he speaks to me, but I feel the venom as he ends me.

I must do whatever it takes to preserve my life, regardless of the meaningless errands that the king insists on sending me on.

The chef's apprentice murmurs beside me as the veiled curtains blow inwards from the soft breeze outside, stirring him whilst he sleeps.

I let out a sigh and climb back under the sheets. I run my fingers down the young man's spine, sidling up to him before returning to my slumber where I am once again lost in dreams.

Fierce burning embers whip up around me, singeing my skin as smoke stings my eyes so sharply that I weep. I'm crying out for help, trying to find her. Nothing can prepare you for the noise when you're inside a burning building – the deafening roar as flames crack around you. I have been here before, visited this memory in my dreams time and time again. The fear grips me the same, and I swear I can feel everything as though I am reliving that day. I call out once more before the ceiling cracks, ready to fall in on itself. Jumping under the table, I curl up in a ball and rock back and forth. I have lost everything on this night. I take hold of the pendant that hangs around my neck and grip it as tightly as I can in my small hand.

When I open my eyes, it is not my chambers I see. The sound of battle rings out as I fire a blast of molten fire towards three soldiers who try to flank me. The blast hits one of them in the face, melting his jaw whilst forming a barrier between me and them. I stare down at my hand, not understanding the power I have just wielded. Another soldier lunges for me and I knock his sword away with my staff before smashing it into his chest. His bones crunch with the force, and the man gasps for air as he slams against the floor. I am surprised by the strength that I possess, and without a moment's hesitation, I aim my hand and raise fire around him. The scent of burning flesh engulfs my nostrils as his wild, panicked screams pierce my ears. Metal against metal rings out as the battle unfolds around me. The black and gold armour of the king's army against a foe that doesn't seem to bear any colours, as if our enemy has pulled together whatever armour and weaponry they could find.

They are disorganised, and our soldiers are slowly gaining the upper hand.

"My queen!" Codrin's deep voice calls from behind me.

The blood of our fallen enemy drenches his dark Elven skin. His words catch me off guard. Did Codrin just call me queen?

"My queen, you should come with me. Our soldiers are taking the keep. If we keep this up, their army will fall."

Something feels strange, and I quickly realise I am not in control of this body. I am a mere passenger, looking out through my own eyes. I know what comes next, I have been here many times. This time, though, just that little bit more is revealed to me.

I try to roar at Codrin, to warn him, but my mouth is sealed shut. My warnings go unheard as I walk towards him. An arrow flies past me, close enough that I feel the brush of its feathers as it ruffles past my hair. With a thud, it buries deep into Codrin's shoulder. Codrin grimaces, raising his hand to snap the arrow before letting out a low growl.

I know the words he speaks next.

"Vireo!" he roars.

Vireo stands in the archway of the door, his second-in-command, Gillam, at his side. He wears the torn green cloak of his dead lover, the one that people of this land tell tales of. How this man has been a constant source of inconvenience to my plans.

Vireo is panting from the steps he has climbed to get here. Gillam rushes forward and throws one of her daggers straight at me. I bring my hand up and project a field of energy which the dagger hits before dropping to the floor. Codrin charges past me, blade in hand as he advances on one of my greatest enemies.

"My queen, go!" he commands. "The wizard should be at the top of the tower!"

The wizard! Yes, the wizard, this is why we are here. The wizard is the key to this. Defeat Jordell and the keep will fall. Jordell – the only person in this land whose power matches, if not surpasses, mine.

Vireo fires another shot into Codrin as the elf slams into him, sending the two crashing to the ground. They begin brawling, their weapons by their sides. Codrin pins Vireo before turning to face me. "Go!" he roars.

I heed his words and begin my ascent up the tower, my heart racing as I frantically draw on my power to reduce the burning sensation in my legs. My chest grows tight as I race upwards, my mind set on what I must do.

Kill the wizard. Kill Jordell.

I wish I could control my body. I know what comes next but I am powerless to stop it. As I reach the opening at the top of the steps, a flash of light blinds me and I raise my hand to shield myself. I swear I see bone through my skin, and I regain composure just in time. Laith swings his sword at me, his face contorted with anger. This man hates me with all the passion of the gods, yet I do not know the reason.

I barely manage to avoid his strike as I swing my staff in defence, which he knocks away. I raise molten fire in my hand and blast the energy towards him but he uses his sword again to block the onslaught. My magic would have melted the steel of a normal sword, yet Laith's is no ordinary sword. It contains a magic never before seen in this land. His blade absorbs my magic before he spins and fires it straight back into me, sending me crashing against the edge of the tower wall.

Rain hammers us, the wind fierce as it lashes my hair

against my face. Laith walks towards me, screaming at me. Oh, how I have wronged this man. His words are muffled and distorted, unclear. I try in vain to focus on what he is saying but the gods are not ready for me to hear this part of my vision. This is often how it works. They give me scraps to go off, like I'm a dog and they're my handlers.

Laith reaches me and drags me from the floor, pinning me against the wall before driving his sword into me. I feel every inch of the blade as it pierces my skin. That's the curse that comes with these visions: I feel everything. The raw emotion, the smells of war, the agonising pain that comes with death.

My vision darkens and a dizziness overcomes me as I cling to life. Laith drives the sword deeper within me before leaning in close to my ear.

"This is for Orjan!"

My mind sparks. I have not heard these words before. For some reason, the gods have seen fit to unmask them. I remain a passenger as the final part of the vision plays out, as Laith roars and topples me over the side of the tower.

I enjoy the weightlessness of the fall. In this moment, it is not panic that overcomes me, but freedom.

I sit bolt upright, gasping for air as I emerge from the dream. My skin prickles with adrenaline as sweat beads down my spine. It takes me a few seconds to realise I am in my chambers and not falling from a tower.

The apprentice lies next to me, gasping for air. My fingers are pressed deeply into his skin, and his face shrivels before me as I draw on the energy within his body. He is too far gone. At this stage, my magic is irreversible, and his skin begins to crack as I absorb the remainder of his life force. He brings his hands to mine but is too weak to pry them away, and his breathing becomes even more laboured until eventually, it stops. His hands fall to the side of mine as he exhales one last gasp of air. I feel revitalised – a little saddened, but revitalised. I had not meant to end the boy's life. He was simply in the wrong place at the wrong time when I woke from my dream.

I let out a sigh. I enjoyed this one. It is a shame he is no longer of this earth. Still, his energy now courses through me and despite his untimely death, today was a good day.

For I have a name. Someone who Laith is clearly fond of. This is the key. I must find the man that will help me prevent my fate.

I must find Orjan. After all, I cannot rule Levanthria if I am unable to cheat death.

3

ORJAN

"The tale of the Baker's Cakes is a tale as old as time. It is a tale of a demon who was able to hide himself in society. Over time the demon was able to use his tricks alongside the pies that he offered to the village, to cast a shroud of magic over the people. This shroud enabled his misdeeds to go notice, for the people were unable to notice that their own children were vanishing. That was until Gregor Yerald landed in Vissel, on this day the demon known as a qallupilluit met its match."

Freya Knach, Tales of Levanthria 142KR.

I COME TO, sniffing the air to be greeted by a stench that forces me to gag. Stale ale and whiskey are on my breath, my mouth dry as I smack my lips together to regain some sort of moisture to them. My clothes are damp from the morning fog that clings low to the ground, and I shuffle upright against the wall as I become aware of my surroundings.

I am under a bridge, like some troll waiting to demand coin from anyone who has the audacity to pass.

A glance at my own scaly hands reminds me that though I may not be a troll, I am a different kind of cursed beast: a fallen knight no longer bound by honour, merely doing whatever it takes to gather coin for my next drink. I'd tried ending it all once or twice, on the darkest nights. I have failed every time, my skin thicker than that of a normal man, which I no longer am.

"Are you okay, mister?"

My eyes stutter and focus on the blurred outline that stands before me. "Go away," I grumble. I am not in the mood for small talk.

"Only, it was cold last night, I came over just in case you were dead. Which you are not." The boy's figure becomes clearer. "Not being funny, but you look like you have been chewed up and spat out from a demon's den."

I sit in the shadows, hiding my true form from him. If he could see me in the light of day, he would be horrified by what he saw.

I can't help but groan as I realise that the boy is still standing there gaping at me. I lean forward from the shadows to reveal my face, knowing that this will be enough to send the scamp running.

The boy gasps and his eyes widen at the monster festering under the bridge. "Your face – what happened to your face?"

"Do you not know the tales of me?" I ask, offering a sick smile as I taunt the boy. But I am impressed by his resolve. Normally at this stage, the revealing of my face is more than enough to ensure I am left to my solitude. Everyone runs, they always do. For some reason this boy remains. His jaw hangs open but he remains nonetheless.

"What tales? Am I meant to have? Are you famous?"

"More infamous," I grumble, a low growl emitting from

my throat. "Have you not heard of the ogre of Osar? The monster that hides in the Mouth of Antar?"

The boy fixes me with an expression of fascination, not fear. "You don't look like an ogre to me."

"What would you call me then?" I rush out of the shadows to reveal my yellow eyes and thick, scaled skin in its entirety. A rush of frustration comes over me when the boy does not follow suit and run.

"You're more lizard than man. You're a lizard man!" The boy looks me over with morbid curiosity. Strangely, he steps closer. "Doesn't matter to me what you are. I work in the shelter down the road. I came here to bring you some soup, so that's what I'm going to do." The boy passes me a small flask.

The bright light from the sun stings my eyes and I take the flask from him before scurrying back into the shadows. My safe place, my solitude. The sun may not cause damage to my skin, but I find it hard to see during daylight. This is why I creep around in the dark, moving from town to town, searching for my next drink.

My fingers are longer than they once were, with claw-like nails protruding from the ends, but I am able to flick the lid off the flask and take in the soup inside. Notes of onions, leeks, and potatoes fill my mouth as an explosion of flavour overcomes me. I let out a groan of appreciation before knocking back the rest of the contents like a ravenous beast.

"Tell me, boy, where is it I find myself?" I smack my lips together, using my forked tongue to capture the soup that escaped my mouth.

"You don't know where you are?"

"Would I have asked if I did?"

"You don't need to be so tetchy, I only came here to give you some soup." The boy's features morph into a frustrated expression. "You're in the dregs of Eltera, not really the kind of place you want to hang around."

Little does he know that this is exactly the kind of place I want to hang around. The more affluent areas in cities are where I draw the most attention. The richer folk would have me impaled on a pike. They have no idea what I have been through, what I have become, yet still they would judge me.

I despise the people of Levanthria. They are far less understanding of people who hail from my kingdom, Rashouya. Still, I cannot return to my people, not in this form, not since the day I was cursed. This is the price I have paid for helping others, for falling into the traps that come with living a life of valour and honour. I had found some form of redemption in helping Zerina and Esara. They brought me back from the brink of death, a life of self-pity and loathing. What thanks do I get for drinking from that damn chalice? My body contorted with agonising pain like I have never felt, my skin transformed, my body stronger but hideous. My mind gone.

I must live with what I did. With what I took from Esara. The way she looked at me when she told me that Ulrik had passed to the afterlife, that I was responsible for it. The venom in her words as she used her glamour magic to take her brother's form. My guilt is like a cloak made of iron.

"As I said, I work at the shelter. Live there, too. It's not the nicest of places but it keeps a roof over my head," the boy continues.

I have no idea why he insists on talking to me. A dull thud pounds away in my head, a reminder of the vast amount of whiskey I drowned myself in the night before. Letting out a low grumble, I show him that I have had enough of his talk.

"A simple 'thank you' would have been enough," the boy

scolds. "Honestly, some people. There's me just about to tell you that if you want a roof over your head rather than a bridge, come to the shelter. It's just past the statue of Lord Zakron."

I can't help but feel like a child being put in his place by his mother. The boy shows me a kindness that I do not deserve.

When he turns to leave, something falls into the mud, but he doesn't seem to notice. I try to call out to him, but I find my tongue rooted to my mouth. If I call out, I'll draw unnecessary attention to myself, something I wish to avoid.

I slump back into the shadows and reach for the bottle next to me.

4

ORJAN

Darkness sets in, and when even my forked tongue cannot pull any extra spirit from the empty whiskey bottle, it's time to leave and find my next drink. I have little coin left, but it's enough to satisfy my thirst in any of the many taverns that lie on these darkened streets.

"Fuck!" I throw the bottle to the ground where it shatters, the noise magnified by the acoustics under the bridge. I bend my neck to the right, then to the left, each time releasing pressure as it cracks like a breaking branch. Stretching out my arms, I let out a low rumble as I stagger to the far side of the bridge where I relieve my full bladder. The ache lessens as my piss strips the moss from the stone. The musk of this place smells like its own hell, and judging by the faecal smell drifting up my nostrils, I can only assume that sewage is nearby.

Something catches my eye: a slight glint magnified by the light of the moon. Curious, I scoop up the item from the ground. Though the item is caked with mud, I can see that it's a pendant. That's when I remember the boy, the one who brought me that nice soup. He did me a kindness. It is only fair that I return his trinket to him. Besides, the shelter is on the way to the inn. There is something about that boy, I think. Something that draws upon long-suppressed memories.

I promise myself that as soon as I get to the inn, it will not be long until that cursed voyage is nothing but a distant memory.

As I walk, the mud feels cold against my clawed toes. What I wouldn't give to feel a pair of boots over my feet once more. The distant noise of dogs barking and the shrieking of cats as they argue with one another rings out. The streets are empty and quiet. Maybe I will stop here for a while after all. I do not like people, but that's not new with the curse. Why change now? A gambling drunk, now a cursed creature. Such a far cry from the honourable knight I once was. If I told anyone of my golden days, they would not believe me. I have fallen so far that not even the gods could bring me back now.

When I reach the shelter, I pull my hood over my head and my scarf over my face to hide my horrific appearance. One person coughs, wrapped in a blanket. Another sips from a bowl of familiar smelling soup.

"I'm looking for a boy," I croak, my throat dry and rasping. I swear for a moment there is a hiss on the end of my tongue, but I put this down to my paranoia.

"Think you are in the wrong place. If it's boys you're after, there is a shop down the road where you can have your fill."

His implications make bile rise to my throat, but I swallow it back down. "He works here, he brought me soup earlier," I growl. "Dropped something. I merely want to give it back."

The balding man drops his head to avoid eye contact with me. Probably the wisest choice he will make all night.

"He's just through there." The other man points to a doorway in the back, his long greasy hair slicked back as best as he could. His eyes are dark, his face wrinkled and worn. "Think he is a bit busy at the minute, though."

I let out another rumble from my throat and head to the doorway. The sooner I give the boy this trinket, the sooner I will be out of here. As I approach, the muffled words in the background become clearer.

"Where is your payment?" a gruff voice bellows.

"I don't have it, I only work here. Bravor should be back soon, I am sure he can help you," the boy's voice replies.

As I enter the room, a large man slams a hand across the boy's face, sending him crashing to the floor with a helpless whimper.

"Please, I don't –"

The man cuts him off and drags him to his feet, gripping him by the scruff of his neck. "You know where he keeps his money. So tell me where it is. Breyton is expecting his payment."

The boy's eyes widen when he spots me. It is enough to distract the brute, who turns his head to follow the boy's gaze.

"Suggest you leave," he warns. "This is nothing to do with you."

"You're right," I hiss. I make it a habit to stay out of others' business. Often, my survival depends upon it.

But when I turn to leave, something sparks in the back of my mind. The boy showed me kindness when few others would, without expecting anything in return. I sigh to myself as I cast my eyes over the man. He is of a larger than average build, and a combination of bulk and muscle strain against the cloth of his shirt. His face is rough like stone, his greying beard full. He is an enforcer for someone.

"However, I have business with the boy," I tell him, holding his gaze.

"Tough guy, are you?" He drops the boy to the floor and clicks his neck as though readying himself for a brawl.

I can forgive him for his idiocy. I am stooping my back heavily out of force of habit. When I stand taller, the man's eyes widen as I overshadow him, even by his own large standard. He doesn't seem too deterred, however, because he reaches to his side and removes a dagger.

"I do not wish to fight, I just want to speak to the boy." I let a rumble escape my throat, enough to warn him of what is to come.

"Piss off, do you know who you are getting in the way of? Breyton will have your guts spewed across the street and your head on a pike."

"I care not for this Breyton. Leave."

The man lunges for me with his knife. I grab hold of his wrist and stop him in his tracks before squeezing it tight enough that his bones crack under the force.

He yelps like a wounded animal and attempts to pull his injured arm away, dropping his dagger in the process. As I pull him closer to my face, I can tell in his eyes he is not used to someone being this much stronger than him.

"Leave!"

I toss him to the side and he staggers through the door, holding his arm tightly with his free hand. "You'll regret this," he warns as he leaves.

The boy looks happy yet concerned as he climbs back to his feet and dusts himself off. "You must be mad! Do you have any idea what you've just done? Breyton will send more of his men here just to teach you a lesson."

"I am just here to give you this, you dropped it earlier." I held my hand out to reveal the pendant.

The boy's eyes seem more drawn to my reptilian hand than to the pendant.

"Well, do you want it back or not?"

"Thank you, I was worried I had lost it." The boy snatches the trinket from my hand and places it into his pocket. "Tell me, what's your name?"

"Why?" I ask. No one has asked me this question for some years.

The boy smiles. "Dunno, just seemed right to ask."

"Orjan. My name is Orjan." Saying my name aloud sounds foreign to me. It has been so long since I last heard it spoken that it feels as though I speak about a stranger, that the name no longer belongs to me.

"I'm Riora. Prefer Rior, though."

"How old are you, boy?"

"Nearly twelve!"

"Well, Rior, I need to be on my way."

"Why not stay for some food first?" he offers. "It's the least I can do."

5

ORJAN

"The Barbaraq's are a fierce race of barbarians that find their honour in conquering and pillaging new lands. They have rarely set foot on the shores of Levanthria but when they do they need to be met with fierceness. For failure to do so will only allow them to think that the kingdom cannot defend itself and this will lead to them pillaging more towns and villages."

Viara Lorentine, Race's of the world, 251KR

Before I know it, I find myself sitting at an old oak table. It is indented from its use, the grain of the wood cracked in multiple places. I fear that if I were to lean on the table too heavily, the legs would break underneath.

"Thank you," I mutter. "Thank you for allowing me to eat with you." It has been so long since I ate in the company of others that I had forgotten how it felt.

"That is no problem at all," Rior's keeper, Preya, answers. "The least we can do, given you helped our Rior." Her curly hair hangs low to her shoulders, her olive skin not matching that of Rior. She wears ragged clothes that hang too loose for her small frame.

"I knew you would understand. Thanks, Preya." Rior beams, grabbing a fresh bread roll and ramming it into his mouth.

Preya, I muse. He calls her by name. She must not be the boy's mother.

"I fear how the Wyverns will react to this." A man stands at the window, staring out at the streets below us. What little hair he has left is a mixture of black and grey, his face one of worry and anguish.

"It was no more than that Wyvern deserved, Bravor," Preya says, placing two bowls of soup on the table. "Roughing up Rior like that."

I look down at the pale green soup and take an inhale, embracing the smell. "Leek and potato?" I ask.

"It is. Mind, you will need to lower your scarf if you are to eat." Preya casts me an enchanting smile. Her warmth towards a total stranger is admirable. She did not have to accept me for dinner, yet she did.

Hesitant, I shuffle in my seat awkwardly. "I am not like others. I look . . . I am different. Please do not be alarmed by my appearance." I lower my mask and prepare myself for Preya to recoil in horror. She does not, though she lets out a short gasp before quickly correcting herself.

"What happened to you? Have you always been a lizard man? Were you born this way?" Rior stares wide-eyed in wonderment as if I am a mythical creature such as a unicorn, not the disfigured beast that I feel like.

"Rior!" Bravor scolds as he takes up a seat next to him, clipping him around the back of the head. "You have been brought up to show more manners than that to our guest." His eyes fix on my scaled face for longer than necessary, but I understand his curiosity. I have seen it more times than I care to recall, but for the first time, I find myself the subject of innocent interest rather than fear.

"It is quite okay." I raise my hand to wave away the boy's direct questioning. "See, it is a tale that I have never really told." My mind races back to the moment where this curse took hold of me, where my body was changed forever. "I was part of a crew that made sail and found ancient waters on the isle of Travertine. Foolishly, I offered to test the waters to trigger their supposed magical properties. Little did I know that drinking from those waters would have such a permanent effect." I omit the part where I lost control of my mind and fatally wounded a good man. Zerina returned me to myself, but it was not soon enough to save Ulrik's life. His death is something that I will bear the guilt of as long as I live.

"Does it hurt?" Rior asks innocently. "Your voice sounds different, it's raspy."

"The transformation itself was the most painful thing I have ever endured," I explain. "My voice sounds different because my body is more reptilian than human now. It does hurt my throat when I talk. I suppose these last few years I have not spoken much."

Rior takes in every word in silent amazement. I take the opportunity to lift the bowl and pour the soup into my mouth, slurping it down. The strong flavour of the leek sets my taste buds into overdrive.

Bravor raises his eyebrow as Preya smiles at my poor table manners. It has been so long since I have sat at a dinner table. "Apologies," I tell them, "my hands make it near impossible for me to use cutlery." I raise a clawed hand to show them.

"You have nothing to apologise for." Preya smiles before lifting her bowl and slurping it as I have – an action that Rior mimics with a gleeful smile.

"Rior says you broke that Wyvern thug's arm," Bravor says.

I nod. "More crushed it than anything."

"I do worry of how they'll react to this," he says. "The Wyverns do not normally harm children, but that said, they are usually acting on orders."

"Maybe we can explain what happened and put it down to a misunderstanding, given our guest is a stranger to this city," Preya offers, gesturing to the others with her eyes for them to start eating their soup. "Sorry for all the questions, Orhan," she adds.

"It's Or-jan, Preya," Rior corrects her.

"It's quite okay, no offence taken." I glance from Preya to Rior. "On either part. Thank you for the invitation for food. I apologise if I have caused any trouble. If anything comes of it, please send them to me. I will make it clear my actions are my own."

"Let's eat up, all this talk of the Wyverns will only serve to raise our anxieties," Preya says whilst fetching a pan of brew.

I raise my hand to stop her pouring into the empty cup in front of me. "I am okay, I prefer my drinks stronger."

Bravor laughs. "A man after my own heart. I have some stronger stuff in the cellar. Drink with me, and then you can sleep in the spare bed."

The thought of sleeping in a bed is tempting. "I do not wish to be an inconvenience."

"It is the least we can do, given the aid you gave to Rior." Preya smiles and reaches across the table to hold Rior's hand.

"Well, that settles it," Bravor says. "I'll go and fetch the wine."

6

MORGANA

Sitting at a table by the balcony, I watch the sun as it rises, its orange glow casting morning light over the kingdom, pushing the shadows backwards like a rescinding ocean that kisses the sand of a beach. My hand is wrapped around the pendant that sits around my neck which brings me comfort as a single tear warms my cheek. The guards drag away the apprentice's body behind me as I sip my fruit-infused tea whilst taking in the warmth that greets my face. My mind searches over my dream again and again. I have seen my end, I have seen my death.

Is everything I have done these last few years, the lives I have devoured, been for no reason? Each move I have made has led to a swelling in my power as I gain a better understanding of the magic that I possess, the magic which no one else can match. When I first arrived in Askela, no one knew my name. I was merely a seer who was in keeping with the king's cousin.

True, I did what I needed to in order to unlock my powers, to let the necromancy surge beneath my skin. Magic takes its toll on the body, punishment for using energy that only the gods should possess. But for me, being able to channel the power of necromancy means I do not have to bear the punishment. I do not need to worry about my body withering away as I draw on my powers. Others pay the price. I barter with their lives to preserve my own.

What is it all for, though? I bring my cup to my pursed lips once more and take another sip of tea, the refreshing citrus flavours bringing my throat to life. I had seen Jareb's fate at the hands of Vireo in a dream before it happened. What happened on the night that Vireo snuffed his life out unfolded exactly how I had foreseen it, exactly how the gods had wanted me to see it. I could have prevented Vireo from forcing his arrow into the side of Jareb's head, and for a brief moment, I had been tempted to. I had grown fond of Jareb during my time with him, but I had seen his death in a vision granted to me by the gods, one that showed me sitting on the throne of Askela as ruler of Levanthria.

True, Eltera's castle is not as grand as the one I have come to call home in Askela, but it is a castle nonetheless, and a thousand miles further from the slums I was born into. Now I must do whatever it takes to seal my fate, to prevent myself from plummeting to my death at the hands of that boy.

"Orjan." The name escapes my lips, rolling off my tongue like silk. I realise I have become lost in my thoughts. I do not know who this man is, but he seems to be important to Laith. If I find him, I may be able to twist my fate as well as turn the tides of the war that is to come. Up until now, I have feared the power that the healer Jordel would come to possess, but as I picture the pure hatred in Laith's eyes, I wonder if perhaps Jordel is not the one I should fear.

Orjan. I muse over his name once more as I stare blankly over the gardens of the castle, the bright green grass shining as the light of the morning breathes new life. Eltera is a smaller kingdom than Askela, but still a kingdom within Levanthria. Within the castle walls and grounds, it would appear somewhat prosperous, but outside these halls, the people struggle to survive the hefty taxes that Codrin enforces in the name of the King's War.

The problem in Eltera lies within its underbelly. A sea of vermin roams these streets in the form of bandits, thieves, and thugs. There is more crime and unrest here than anywhere across Levanthria. And now, King Athos wants me to put a stop to it.

I've sent spies here, of course, as I have throughout Levanthria. But for the past year, my messengers have returned from Eltera bloodied and beaten – and my spies do not return at all. Someone runs these streets from the shadows, and I intend to find out who.

I take another sip of my tea and savour the tinge of citrus that sits on my tongue before swallowing it. It brings a crisp freshness to my mouth, and I feel as though it energises me, readies me to deal with my tasks of the day.

As I make to leave the room, I glance at the now empty bed. All that remains is the cindered ashes of the cook's apprentice. I find myself smiling as his life energy courses around my body, tingling in very part of me. Thanks to him, I can access my magic today without fear of consequence to my body.

When I enter the great hall, I find it lacklustre in comparison to the great hall in Askela. Self-serving portraits hang from the walls, each one a ghastly painting of the lords that have inhabited this castle. Judging by the large noses and receding hairlines, they are all descendants of the same family. The metallic frames are rusted and some of them hang at an off-angle, the dust that clings to them betraying their neglect. On one painting of a younger ward who seems to have more in common with a weasel than with his forbears, the corner is blemished, and I am unable to tell if this is age or mould.

"Lady Morgana, you're awake. I have had some food prepared for us." A portly, clean-shaven man dressed in a dark green tunic stands from the table to greet me.

I glance pointedly at the sword sheathed by his side. "Tell me, Wistler, do you fear me that much?" I stride over to the table and sit at a chair that has already been pulled out for me by a kitchen boy, and I smile as I reach for a piece of groa fruit from a colourful platter. When I bring it to my mouth, Wistler's eyes widen as if in anticipation. "Do I need to worry that this groa is poisoned, Wistler?"

Wistler struggles to find his words. "My lady, I wish only to see that it is satisfactory and to your taste." He bows his head and sits opposite me, reaching for some fruit himself.

If Wistler were not my host, I would send him away; I do not wish to keep company with such a snivelling, cowardly man. Wistler has not earned this castle. He has not worked a single hard day in his life. Unlike myself, he has been given his riches, according to whatever agreement he has with the king. He does not know the true value of the gold and treasures that he keeps in his vaults. If the rumours are true, Wistler's wealth far outweighs that of most people across Levanthria. By all rights, Eltera should be thriving under his hand. Instead, I find myself in a city where vermin roam the streets and call themselves kings and queens.

Wistler gapes at me as I chew my groa fruit, a frustrated

noise leaving his nostrils as he breathes heavily. I laugh to myself. Is this where he gets the name Wistler from?

On the far side of the hall, I notice a strange looking axe perched on a plinth. It is a two-handed great axe, its wooden handle carved with symbols that are not Levanthrian, or even Elvish for that matter.

"Where is that from?" I ask, walking over to inspect the weapon. Its head is made of obsidian, the edges of which are serrated.

"It is a Barbaraq great axe. A gift to Eltera, years past." He walks over to join me.

I stare at my reflection in the obsidian. *Barbaraqs.*

"Is everything to your satisfaction?"

I swear I see his hand tremor as he brings his fruit to his mouth to take a bite. Even the way he eats is infuriating. You would think with all his wealth, he would have grown to have better table manners.

"It is. Let's get to the business at hand, shall we?" My words are short and curt. I wish to spend as little time as possible with Wistler's pointed face and wheezing breath.

"Please tell me how I can aid you today."

I return to my seat at the table, and Wistler joins me. "There is a power struggle, my lord. You must have noticed it. Or do you never leave your castle walls?" I relish the panic that flashes across Wistler's face.

"The last few years have been most unkind to Eltera," he says. "Our once prosperous kingdom has fallen on hard times."

"Tell me, Wistler, when *was* the last time you left these walls?"

"Eltera has become a dangerous place, Morgana. It was only two years ago that a witch slaughtered my men whilst awaiting trial."

I have heard the stories of this witch and the things she has done, and I must admit, I envy her power. With her infamous fury, Zerina would certainly make a great addition to my ranks. She is said to have brought down an entire ship belonging to the King's Fleet, leaving only a few to tell the tale.

"Since the witch trials, the streets have become a cesspit!" Wistler continues. "Gangs of men and women have taken the streets, organised and mobilised by people I do not know. It is a wonder they haven't tried to storm the castle! It is only trade that allows my men to leave the castle to gather supplies. If a soldier sets foot outside, they are targeted, assassinated, or beaten in the streets like commoners." Wistler blows out his cheeks as his face reddens, puffing his chest out defiantly before adjusting his tunic to regain some composure. His blustery excuses do not fool me. I know it is his cowardice that has led his kingdom to its current state.

"So, you allowed your kingdom to succumb to the rule of common folk. How does it feel to know that you have yielded the power that your family worked so hard for? How they must be turning in their graves." I don't bother to hide the venom on my tongue.

"Morgana, I have had little choice in the matter. When the witch –"

I cut him off by rising to my feet, my chair grinding against the wooden floor. "You had every choice any other person in your position would've had. You chose not to bring your people to heel and look at the chaos that it has brought to your lands. Your people do not respect you. They are no longer even your people, are they? They belong to someone else. And as a result, you have jeopardised the King's War." I feel my temper flaring and I cannot bear to be around this petulant man any longer. It is his fault that I am here in this wretched, rat-infested city.

I can feel myself plummeting to my death from that tower. I have much bigger problems to worry about than Wistler's failures – but for now, I must do as the king commands.

7

ORJAN

"Ironite ore has said to be wanted by countries all over the world due to the magical properties they are said to contain. Those magical properties are believed to be what enables armour forged from the metal within to be so strong and dextrose."

Jonah Viergen, Minerals and Ore's of the lands, 260KR

THE NEXT MORNING after the best night's rest I've had in a long time, I head to the market with Rior to gather some fresh produce for today's broth. Bravor seemed on edge about Rior travelling alone after what happened yesterday with the Wyvern thug. I felt it only right that I escort Rior to the markets and back. Once he is back at the shelter, I will make my leave. I've already spent more time than I intended in this city. It is time for me to move on to the next wretched town and find a new hole to drink in.

The brightness of the morning brings with it a lack of shadows for me to hide in. I ensure my scarf remains pulled up over my nose, hiding my monstrous features from the world. But I cannot hide my yellow eyes.

To our right, a man pushes a cart with what smells like fresh bread. A pang of hunger hits me in the stomach like a blow from a mace. Not far behind him, a young girl carrying a fishing rod twice her size skips down the cobblestones with not a care in the world.

"Tell me, Rior, how far is it until we reach the markets?" I glance at the whistling young boy who escorts me as if it is he who is my guardian. An old feeling tugs at my soul. He reminds me of Laith, and the thought causes a knot of guilt to form in my stomach.

"Not far, it's near the outer walls of Eltera. Since the Wyverns took over the city, they moved it as far away from the castle gates as possible." Rior resumes his whistling.

"Eltera," I think out loud as I ponder the name. How is the name so familiar?

Rior casts me a puzzled look. "Do you not recall your conversations with Bravor last night?"

"I drink to banish my memories, they are of no use to me. It matters not where I find myself, as long as –"

"Long as you can find your next drink," Rior finishes my sentence with a smug grin as if he has me figured out already. "You know, I have been helping at the shelter as long as I can remember. You're not the first drunkard to come stumbling in. I've heard your story time and time again, except normally they don't have scales."

A low grumble rises in my throat. "Mind your tongue, boy." The boy is sharp, and more than happy to speak his mind. It is a trait I admire, but one that I must rein in.

"I didn't mean any harm by it, jeez. No need to get all rumbly with me."

Again, the boy reminds me of Laith, who was my squire

for six years. Laith travelled with me across these lands as I trained him in what it means to be a knight. How to speak, how to eat, how to ride a horse, how to fight. The time spent with him gave me a purpose in life. It is only natural that a knight comes to care for his squire as if he were his own blood.

I find my mind spiralling into the void of memories. Laith *was* like a son to me, yet still I cast him away when I found myself drowning in shame. Bloodied and beaten at the hands of that bastard, Vireo, humiliated and dumped at the gates of Askela as if I were nothing more than shit that needed scraping from the streets.

People laughed at me, people taunted me, goaded me. Not one person offered me help or shelter in my time of need. As a Rashouyan knight, I found the shame this brought me unbearable. Unable to beat a nobleman in combat over a gambling debt I did not remember wagering. That is the curse of drink and games.

"You okay, Orjan?" Rior elbows me in the leg, and I snap back from my thoughts.

"You remind me of someone I once knew."

As we near the market, the day breathes life into the mud-lined streets. Buildings stand in crumbled states of disrepair, and every face seems drawn with misery. There is no idle talk, no cautious laughter as townsfolk trudge to their destinations with bent heads.

"Tell me, Rior, how was it you came to be with your keepers?"

Rior casts me another puzzled look. "I have no keeper. Bravor has always looked over me, providing I help him at the shelter. I wouldn't say he is my keeper, though."

"Does he give you food, a roof over your head, and the clothes that you wear?"

"Well, I suppose so, but it's Preya who provides me with food and clothes. I can come and go as I like."

"Like a stray cat then," I tease.

"No, not like a cat," Rior snaps at me. "I may be young, but I am free."

"I only jest, Rior, I mean you no ill will." I raise my hands in mock surrender. Rior is small, but I wouldn't be surprised if he threw a punch at me.

"They have shown me kindness where others wouldn't. I'm not from Eltera, you see. Truth is, I don't know where I am from. I was dumped at an orphanage south of the Pendaran Hills. I ran away and this city was the first place I found. I was living under the same bridge where I found you when Preya found me."

"So they adopted you?" I ask, my lips smacking together from the dryness. Another strong smell drifts pass me, this time it is fish. It sends my stomach into a frenzy. We must be getting close to the market now.

"If you want to think of it like that, suppose they did. Wyverns had already taken over the city when I arrived. Bravor told me it was because of what happened at the witch trials. Come on, the market is up this way."

An audible growl emits from Rior's stomach, loud enough for him to look embarrassed by it.

"Hungry? Did you not eat before we left?"

Rior shoves his hands into his pockets, looking uncomfortable. "Well, supplies are running short these days. It's not Preya's fault, it's those Wyverns. Nothing short of sluggers, them. We buy the vegetables that are left over, the vendors keep it to the side. They know we're providing food for those who can't afford it, so they give it to us for a fair price."

I can't help but wonder how these Wyverns have come

to ascertain such a hold over this city. Why the people have simply allowed this astounds me.

"Where are the kingdom's guards?"

"Holed up there." Rior points to the circular castle that sits in the distance, atop a small keep overlooking the city. Perfectly placed for a defensive siege. "Cowards have been hiding up there ever since the witch trials. That bastard Breyton saw an opportunity and took it. Now he runs things around here and Lord Wistler has left us to rot. If people don't do what Breyton commands, they tend to not stay alive for much longer. It's fear that keeps this place going now, nothing else."

I ponder this until I hear another grumble emit from Rior's empty stomach.

"Come, boy. I find myself hungry too." I remove my small purse from my pocket. Though the coins I earned from odd bounty work here and there have run low, I toss a silver coin to Rior. "For the food yesterday, and the bed."

His eyes widen before he gives me a smile that threatens to split his cheeks. "Thank you."

When we reach the hustle and bustle of the market, I spot a fruit and toss another coin to Rior. "Go get us the juiciest apples you can find. I need to take a piss. Meet me back here in a moment. I don't want to get too familiar with these crowds."

Rior nods with gratitude and heads off to the vendor whilst I make my way towards an alley to relieve myself of my aching. When I return, Rior is not there. After a few more minutes of waiting, I cannot help but notice a crowd gathering near the fruit vendor.

I curse. How has he managed to create a commotion in the few moments he was out of my sight? I prefer to keep from the crowds, but I have no choice but to head towards whatever the ruckus is. I am surprised by the pang of concern I feel about the boy's wellbeing.

There is hushed silence amongst the crowd, an air of uncomfortable restraint. An odd cough escapes as they stand and gawp. Without uttering a word, I part the crowd to either side of me so I can see what is happening.

Rior is on the ground, clasping a reddened cheek as a small cloud of dust settles around him. A brute towers over him – the same man who paid a visit to the shelter the previous day. His injured arm is in a splint, but he grabs hold of Rior's arm with his free hand and drags him to his feet as if he weighs nothing.

"You shit!" he snarls, teeth bared as he pulls Rior's face towards his own. Rior stares back, undeterred. "My arm is fucked because of you." He throws Rior into the fruit stand, sending the apples splaying across the dirt-ridden ground, then pulls out a dagger, ready to strike.

Gasps ring out amongst the crowd, but no one steps forward to lend Rior aid. They simply stand and watch, their lack of action making them complicit in his beating.

People grunt and groan with displeasure as I force my way through the crowd just as the man lunges forward with his blade. *Shit, he is actually going to kill the boy.*

I grab hold of his arm just in time and stop him in his tracks. The gasps from the crowd grow even louder as if they are shocked by my action and not by their own inaction.

"I think you will find it is I who is responsible for your arm," I snarl.

The man turns and looks me in the eye, and I dead-stare him. He cannot see my face under my scarf, but I am growling underneath. That threatening rumble returns to my throat. His eyes widen, and before he has a chance to think of his next step, I slam my free arm into the back of his elbow. A howl of pain escapes his mouth as his arm breaks at the point of contact. Blood sprays from where a bone now protrudes from his skin. Without hesitation, I slam my fist into his face, and even when his nose explodes, I do not relent. I grip him to stop him from falling and keep him in place as I strike him again and again. My anger drives me forward with each strike until nothing remains but bloodied pulp and a lifeless man.

I toss him to the floor and offer a hand to Rior. A panicked expression is frozen into his face like a painting.

"You do not need to fear me, Rior, that man was about to end your life. He did not deserve his own."

"You have no idea what you have done," Rior warns. His gaze shifts over my shoulder, and I know in an instant that this fight is far from over.

I turn to see half a dozen men rushing towards me, all with weapons varying from daggers, swords, maces, and axes. They intend to make an example of me.

Well, I intend to make an example of them.

8

MORGANA

"Open the gates!"

The guards stutter at my command, but I stand undeterred by the world that awaits me outside these walls.

"Lady Morgana, wait! You do not understand." Wistler tries in vain to slow my haste, but I care not for the words that fall from his lips. His face is red and blotchy as he scurries to keep up with me.

"I understand clearly, Wistler. You have let these people run amok. They do not know fear like they should."

"They do, the people do. The Wyverns govern with it. The people who are in command out there."

I look to the skies and wish for the gods to strike this man down where he stands. It is something I'd consider myself, but that would not work well with the bureaucracy of Levanthria. Such tales could stop my ascension. True, I hold power, but even I know that a leader needs followers.

"You allow them to command a name as if they are some faction worthy of anything other than the dungeons," I continue. "It is these Wyverns who need to know fear, this is the only way you will bring your people back to heel."

"What do you intend on doing out there?" Wistler snivels.

"I intend to show them fear. It is the only way we will get Eltera back to how it once was. This is the kingdom where ironite armour is forged, is it not?" And now my true purpose is revealed to the Lord of Eltera: it is armour and weaponry that I desire.

"At least take a couple of my men with you."

"Do you feel that I need protection, Wistler? Do you consider me a mere damsel needing help?" My eyes flare and a surge of magic shivers through my body, the raw energy raising my hair from my head.

"No, not at all, Morgana. I mean no offence."

I stare at the guard who stands by the gate, and he gestures for it to be opened. Chains begin to draw, and the grinding noise tells me that these gates are not opened often. I stand impatiently as the gates open at a sluggish pace.

"I shall be back before long, hopefully with some good news," I announce.

I take a step from the castle and begin my descent into town, my dress trailing through the dirt as I walk. I am not long into my walk when an unpleasant smell greets me. Sewage, waste, and death is all I can liken it to. The slums of Askela are lavish compared to Eltera's, and I find myself shocked once more by the state the kingdom has fallen into. These Wyverns have a lot to answer for, and I seek to find them as quickly as possible so I can return to Askela and plan for the Great War that is coming, equipped with superior ironite armour and weapons.

I find my mood darkened with my mind fixed on Laith

and the anger he shows towards me as he kicks me over the edge of the castle tower to my death. In truth, it is all I have been thinking about for the past few moon cycles, since my visions revealed Laith as the person responsible for the end of my life. The fact that I am stuck here dealing with Wistler's foolish problems instead of seeking a solution to my own fate grates on my nerves.

As I head towards the markets, eyes follow me in my fine red dress. Everyone I see looks pale and gaunt, as if the sun does not shine light on the people here. I have seen people in the dungeons appear in a better state of health than some of these. The clothes they wear are dirty and torn, and I can't help but question how these people are surviving.

Still, it is access to the forge that I need, and to gain that, I must find whoever is in charge of the Wyverns. The markets are often the best place to gather information. I have no doubt that someone will loosen their tongue with a little persuasion.

The odious smell makes me gag a little, and for a moment I worry that I might empty the contents of my stomach. I hold it back though, thinking of the scalding bath I will take when I return to the castle to remove the stench that clings to me.

My mood lifts slightly when the market comes into my line of sight, and I spot a crowd gathered with raised voices. I head to it at once, eager to see what it is that has so many people in an uproar.

A lifeless corpse lies slumped on the ground, his face beaten and unrecognisable. Two other men lie groaning in pain, one holding his leg, another holding his hand to the thick gash down his cheek. Four men are attempting to box in a hooded figure who stands taller than all of them, his face covered by a scarf. Something doesn't seem right about this man. His eyes are yellow, his skin indescribable at this distance. I would need to be closer to see, I want to be closer to see.

A brute attempts to take the yellow-eyed man's head with a sword, but the hooded figure traps his attacker's arm before slamming his head into his face. He brings the man's arm down and drives the sword he is holding into one of the other men's stomachs. The snapping of the attacker's wrist causes him to scream out in pain and the tall man growls. It is a noise I have never heard come from a man. Another five men and women enter the fray to try and subdue their quarry.

One of them launches a dagger that embeds into the yellow-eyed man's leg. He growls at them with fury as he reaches down and pulls it free. Blood streams down his leg, but he does not seem deterred by his ailment. Enraged, the hooded man removes a weapon from his side, and I am amazed to realise that he unleashed this destruction up until now without use of a weapon. He roars as he swings his mace, connecting it with the side of a man's head. A sickening crunch causes the crowd to groan.

The hooded figure's attackers circle him. Now I count six in total. It would seem these people are like a hydra; for every one he strikes down, two more rise up. Blood decorates the ground around them, moans and groans escaping the lips of those lucky enough to still cling to life. Two of the attackers prod the air with their pikes from a safe distance, but the strange man easily parries them away, all the while emitting a low grumbling noise from under the scarf he hides behind.

"Steady, we attack together. Breyton will not be happy unless we bring his head," a woman commands. She is a strong, well-built woman, and appears to hold some form of rank over the others. Her dirty-blond hair is matted with her comrades' blood, a section of which is shaved to her scalp, revealing a serpentine tattoo. Judging by the dragon inked into her skin, I assume these are the very Wyverns that I have come here looking for. How delightful.

The hooded figure staggers slightly and, sensing an opportunity, the leader of the group steps forward and shoves her pike into his side. He growls with pain but looks at his attacker with vengeance. He yanks the pike from his own flesh, then uses it to swing the woman to the side. She clatters into the crowd, sending a score of bodies tumbling. This man is incredible, and I know what I must do, what I want to do.

I draw my hood and step forward from the crowd, a surge of magic coursing up my body and down my arm. I move my fingers to ensure the magic keeps moving. I have found letting it remain in one place inflicts more pain on me if I am not channelling through another body. A green blast of raw magic sparks from my fingertips and into the back of one of the Wyverns. He is knocked forwards into the path of the man with the scarf, whose eyes widen like a ravenous monster ready to feast on its prey. He brings his mace down onto the skull of the man standing before him. The Wyvern begins to convulse before dropping to the ground, blood cascading from his eyes and ears.

"What the fuck was that!" the leader cries as she gathers herself from the crowd she was hurled into.

"It's a witch!" another brute calls as he points his pike at me.

A witch! How dare he. I am much more than a mere witch. My power has already far exceeded my own expectations.

"I think you will find I am a sorceress!" I glower as I stare into the man's soul, then begin to channel further magic. I aim both of my hands, one at the hooded figure and one at the balding fat brute before me. The spark of energy sends a flutter inside my chest as I connect with both men. The yellow-eyed man drops to his knees, growling as he clutches his injured side. I focus on the man pointing the pike at me and a look of terror overcomes him. He drops his weapon and clasps his hand to his side as blood begins to flow through the gaps of his fingers.

"What are you doing to him? Stop!" the leader demands, her voice ringing out from the dispersing crowd. They do not wish to see the spectacle now that they know magic is involved, especially dark magic.

With a flick of my wrist, I fire a jolt of magic at the now injured man, having transferred the hooded man's injury to him. It connects with his face and there is a sickening crack as his head snaps. This isn't the first time I have used that spell, but it is the first time I have used it in open combat.

I count three people remaining, and with two against one, I find these odds much fairer than previously. As I dash forward, the leader of the group panics, evidently not expecting such a move.

"You're all cowards," I snarl as I clasp either side of her head. I need to replenish the magic stores within my body if I am to prevent myself from succumbing to the aftereffects of magic use. Her eyes meet mine and her face contorts in agony as I absorb the life force within her. Her face thins and becomes gaunt until it resembles that of a rapidly ageing woman. The sensation in my hands is as if they are attempting to propel themselves from one another as the pressure builds. I maintain my focus and fight to keep them in the same place, all the while the pressure growing, causing my hands to vibrate intensely.

I know what comes next. I turn my face to the side as the woman's head explodes from the pressure, her flesh and blood spraying over me. I feel alive, as though a freshness has taken over me. I pant heavily as I gather myself from the life force I have just absorbed. It is as though the coldest water has washed over me and my skin prickles with the sensation. I embrace the feeling, devouring every moment.

The remaining two men drop their weapons and bolt into the crowd. They have seen sense, and I have caused enough of a spectacle for one day.

"You there. Follow me, before more people arrive." I beckon the hooded figure towards me. I have channelled enough energy for one morning, and although I could continue, I wish not to draw further eyes upon myself or my magic. I have done enough for people to recognise who I am, and this will no doubt reach whoever is in charge of these Wyverns.

Breyton. The name rings in my mind as I remember the woman speaking his name as if he commanded some form of influence over them. "Come!" I command once more to the yellow-eyed man who stands in shock, blood of his enemies pooled around him.

He searches around him as if looking for something as blood drips from the spiked ball of his mace.

"If you wish to see how I use my magic on those who disobey, then I suggest you stay where you are."

The man remains rooted to the spot, looking for something.

"You must not value your own life. Come, I want you to hear what I have to offer."

The man's eyes meet my own and I am mesmerised by the deep-yellow colour. This man intrigues me.

Finally, he takes a step towards me. He looks at his legs,

no doubt shocked and confused by the lack of pain that he should be feeling from his injuries.

"Where is it you take me?" he grumbles, a hoarse husk in his voice.

I point toward Lord Wistler's home at the top of the keep. "You shall take refuge in the castle."

9

ORJAN

T he woman's magic chills me to my core and my instinct is to put as much distance between her and myself as possible. But as I eye the exploded remains of the Wyvern woman's head splattered at my feet, I realise I must follow this sorceress if I hope to escape a similar fate.

Rior is nowhere in sight, and I can only hope he made it quietly to safety – somewhere far away from me. I fear the retribution he will face just by his association with me. With one last glance into the crowd, I fall in step behind the witch, vowing to return as soon as I can to ensure Rior's wellbeing.

The sorceress walks ahead of me, her red dress soaked in the crimson blood of our enemies. The last time I saw such powerful magic, Zerina was laying waste to a ship and its crew, her fury showing no bounds. This sorceress, however, showed refined control of her powers, which I did not think possible. There was no anger in her face. Instead, it was enjoyment that cascaded over her as she took the lives of our attackers.

I shudder at the thought of the magic, given that it was an ancient Elven curse that left me with my ailment. My chest still pounds with the blast of adrenaline from the fight. I am much stronger than most, but even by my standards I could not have maintained my defensive formation for much longer. If not for this sorceress, I may not have survived that fight. Once I have the shelter of the castle walls, I will thank the sorceress properly, then return to Eltera to find Rior.

"Open the gates!" the sorceress bellows, her words echoing around us. The wrought-iron gates begin to slowly open and it is clear that she commands some form of power over these people. After seeing her magic, it is little wonder why.

"What have you done?" A well-spoken, portly man stands before the sorceress. His face is reddened with the blotches of excess drink, the redness and swelling in his nose a tell-tale sign.

"I have simply done what I must," the sorceress says as she walks past through the courtyard and towards the entrance to the castle with a dismissive look.

I follow her, looking at the man as I pass. I tower over him by a good two feet and his eyes widen in apprehension as he looks me up and down. I laugh to myself and follow the tracks of my rescuer.

"Someone fetch me a towel!" the woman commands as we enter through the large wooden doorway into a grand entrance, the likes of which I have not seen in many years. "Tell the maids to start a bath for me."

We travel up a flight of stairs and walk down a large stone walkway into what I assume is the main hall of the castle. The woman stops and turns to face me, lowering her hood. The red ringlets of hair that escape down to her shoulders are matted with blood, her emerald-green eyes contrasting with the crimson splatters on her face. Despite the morbid sight, I find her gaze enchanting as she looks me over.

"Well, are you not an interesting specimen." She smiles, examining my yellow eyes and scaled skin. A maid rushes to her side and begins to pat at her face with a wet towel. She sighs and grabs hold of the towel before wiping it across her own face.

"Tend to my bath," she commands, and the maid bows her head before scurrying away, her faint steps echoing in the empty room.

The sorceress continues to wipe away the blood until her pale skin emerges from a beautiful face decorated with freckles. She offers me the towel, but I shake my head.

"Lower your scarf. I want to see your face." Her tone is measured but unreserved. I am in no doubt that it is a command, not a request.

"I assure you that you do not."

She places her fingers on the edge of my scarf and I feel a jolt of magic at her touch. I can't remember the last time a woman touched my face, and I feel threatened by it. I growl from my throat to warn of my displeasure but the woman is unfazed. And why would she be intimidated by the likes of me? I just watched her stay our attackers like they posed no danger at all to her, and she smiled whilst she did it.

I pull back, but the woman takes hold of my scarf and lowers it. My full scaled face is revealed to her, and she takes in my reptilian eyes, my pointed, jagged teeth. I grumble again, feeling uncomfortable as she inspects me.

"Fascinating. You clearly like your ale, and you are in need of a bath. Your smell is quite repulsive. But there is something that I have no doubt you can help me with."

She circles me like a beast stalking its prey before devouring it. I wonder if she is contemplating using that magic of hers on me, and I look around the room to plan my escape.

"You're a tall man, if I can call you that. Yet, would I be correct in saying you are hunched?"

"You would be correct."

"Just what are you?"

I can feel her gaze rake my back and her behaviour begins to exasperate me. "Cursed. I am cursed. Listen, thank you for helping me, but I need to go find my friend –"

"So you were once a man?"

"I was – I am still a man. My lady, if I may, I have matters I need to attend to most urgently," I press, my discomfort growing.

"Remove your tunic," she commands. "Well, what remains of it, anyway."

"No!" I growl. "I must make my leave."

The woman's eyes flare with anger and I sense energy coursing around her as she flexes her powers.

"I want to see you entirely. Do as I ask, and I will help you in your endeavour. I assure you of this." Having borne witness to what this woman is capable of, I do not wish to fall foul of her. Left with little choice, I nod.

She flicks her hand, using her magic to slice my torn tunic as if she holds a blade. I grab hold of my shoulder and tear the clothes down, displaying my scaled torso and the reason why my back is hunched.

"Is that a shell?" The woman smiles again as she moves behind me, amazed at the spectacle before her.

I have never thought of it as a shell, but given my scaled appearance, it is little wonder why she would refer to it this way. In the years that have passed since this curse was inflicted upon me, the skin covering my back has become harder and harder. I have stood in front of mirrors to see what it is that was happening to me, and watched as over time, the hardened surface stretched over the length of my back until it stopped just above my buttocks.

Without asking, she places her hand on my back and runs her fingers over me. It is a dulled sensation, like my skin truly lies behind the thickened mass that has formed there.

"Does it affect your movement?"

"It does." A sense of shame falls over me. Does this woman intend on having my head and displaying me like some kind of trophy for all to see? What is it she desires from me?

She trails her fingers over me until she stands in front of me once more, dragging her nails lightly over the scales on my chest. Then she presses more firmly, as if testing the strength of my hide. "I will have the maids wash you, and the dresser will fetch you a new tunic. Then you will go through every detail that led to your condition."

"I have something I need to tend to," I remind her.

"You will do this for me, and then I will help you. Tell me, what is your name? I am Morgana."

I must go along with this if I am to find Rior. "My name is Orjan."

A panicked look falls across Morgana's face. She stumbles away from me, a vulnerability overcoming her that I did not expect.

"It can't be. You – you're –" she makes distance between us before a flicker of magic forms in her hand. Within a moment, a green blast of energy smashes into my chest and I crumple to the floor, my body contorting with pain. When this curse enveloped my body, it was the most painful thing

I had ever felt. Until now. I am powerless to stop my body convulsing as needle-sharp pain pricks my body all over, my muscles contorting tightly, causing my limbs to twist at unnatural angles. It is as though an unseen force manipulates my body, squeezing me tightly enough to force the air from my chest. All I can muster is an agonising grunt as pain erupts all over me as though my muscles are tearing throughout my body. Like flames creeping up a pyre, the force surrounds me as I gasp for air.

"Guards! Guards!" Morgana's muffled words ring out in the hall, and I hear sudden footsteps approaching.

I attempt to press myself up from the floor, but my arms buckle underneath me and my face smashes into the floor. My nose throbs from the impact as a pool of my own blood begins to cascade from it. "Why?" I stammer. "I have done you no wrong."

The blurred frame of Morgana stands over me as I howl with pain. Just a moment ago she was looking over me with fascination, offering to help me. My mind races, trying to decipher what changed, but I have no answers.

I feel my arms pulled behind me and bound with rope, the tightness of which causes me to wince as it breaks into my skin. I fall limply against the guards as they heave me to my feet.

"Take him to the dungeon!" Morgana snarls. I feel a blow to the back of my head, and as Morgana's blurred image fades, I greet the darkness.

10

MORGANA

"In a time long a go humans were not considered the only race to walk these lands. Elves, Fae, Dwarves, Gnomes and Orks are said to have once inhabited this world. Although there remains limited evidence other than those in scriptures of all these races, it is known that there are sections of the world that remain unexplored. It is here where some of these races may live."

Heldara Berein, Scholar to the temple of Orion, 206KR

HOW THE GODS TAUNT ME. First, they provide me visions of my own death. Now they bring me face-to-face with someone who is key to my demise.

At first, I found his struggle alluring, clearly using drink to cope with the curse that afflicts him. But when the beast told me his name, my body went cold with shock. Now the warmth of the bath scalds my skin, palliating the cold. I inhale the lavender-infused vapours which help settle my nerves, and my heart slows to a regular thrum whilst the pulsating feeling in my head subsides. I slide further into the bath, allowing the water to cascade over my head. Under the surface, I let out the loudest scream that I can muster. Pockets of air leave my mouth as I roar into the void, unable to centre my thoughts. I feel a sting up my nostrils as air forces its way in, causing a pressurised sensation to the forefront of my head and behind my nose. I reach for the side of the copper tub and hoist myself to the surface, panting heavily whilst I gather my thoughts.

I had a plan for the beast. I had an idea for how I was going to use him. In learning his name, I let my guard slip, let him see my fear of him. I reacted with haste, and attacking him and sending him to the dungeons isn't likely to have helped me recruit him in my endeavour to rid Eltera of these so-called Wyverns.

I cannot remember the last time I cast my magic through fear, and I assume it was only his reptilian-like scales that allowed him to survive the attack. That same spell has reduced countless men and women to ashes, yet he endured it.

It is clear that the gods have a plan for me. Why else would they do this to me, why else would they let our paths collide like this? My meeting with Orjan was fated. Now I just need to find out why. Somehow, he is connected to Laith.

The problem with visions is that they show you a destination, but not the path that leads there. It is through these visions that I have been able to manipulate my fate to rise to the power that I already have. I have cheated death once before. How hard could it be to do so a second time?

Killing Orjan seems like the easiest option, but Laith's words from my vision drives through me like his blade to my stomach.

"This is for Orjan." The words stumble from my lips as I

stare into nothing. Killing him would certainly drive a man as loyal as Laith to want revenge against me. Do they even know each other? I have so many questions.

Shortly after dressing, there is a knock at my door. I can tell by the weakened, rushed tapping who it is in an instant, and I let out a sigh.

"You may enter."

Wistler scurries in and bows his head to me as he steps into my chamber, his mere presence causing me to shudder. The man is a snake.

"What is it you want, Wistler?"

As lord of this kingdom, it is telling that he does not challenge me despite my petulance. A lord with a backbone would have already squashed the leaders of the Wyverns to set an example for anyone else with ideas of rebelling.

"I have had word from the streets of Eltera." Wistler stands with his hands behind his back like a servant instead of a lord. "The Wyverns are not happy with the disrespect shown to their men and women. They are planning to storm the castle and overthrow the kingdom in its entirety."

"Are the stories spreading about the chaos we brought down on them?" I ask as I turn to take in the fresh air from the balcony. The air tastes so much cleaner here than it did in the markets.

Wistler moves beside me, somewhat confused by my reaction. "Are you not concerned about the consequences of your actions? Maybe you misheard me –"

"*My* actions? It was not I who started the fight. I merely saw to recruit someone who I thought would be able to help us in our endeavour of regaining control over Eltera. Is that not what I was sent here by the king to do? Regain control of the kingdom you have lost?" A wry smile curls up in the corner of my mouth and I can sense the fear oozing from Wistler like a pious pimple.

"Oh, and your new pet is awake," Wistler says. "What did the beast do to you? Who is he?" He is unable to hide his eagerness for information.

I ponder on my thoughts for a moment, his name sitting on my lips as I wonder whether to reveal it or not. "Orjan."

"The disgraced knight of the Rashouyan empire?" Wister looks surprised.

That piques my interest. Maybe through knowledge of his former life, I can learn of his link to Laith. "A disgraced knight?"

"He left Rashouya in shame, cast out for reasons I do not know. They say he was on some self-proclaimed quest to regain his honour so he could return to their lands. He was last seen in Askela, bested in combat at the hands of Vireo over a gambling debt, beaten and humiliated."

That doesn't explain how he ended up within the walls of this castle, inflicted with such a terrible curse. What did he do to warrant such a miserable existence? What is it he has done to anger the gods so much that they would transform him into such a ferocious creature?

"I have it on good word that when Orjan was beaten in the street like a pauper, he was not travelling alone," Wistler adds, gleeful to know something that I don't. "He had a squire."

It has been years since the night Jareb died at the hands of Vireo, the same night when I first came across Laith as he bravely endured Codrin's lashes. This is the link. This is how the two know one another, I am certain of it.

"Thank you, Wistler." I smile at him in a pleasing manner. For once, the fool has served a purpose. I nod politely to him and turn to leave.

"Where is it you head, Lady Morgana?" Wistler asks through rushed breath.

"I need to go and speak with our creature in the dungeon. I know precisely what to do with him."

11

ORJAN

When I come to, I raise my hand to the ache in the back of my head. Wincing, I roll onto my back before forcing myself to sit upright, feeling as if I have been beaten by a hundred fists. My curse exaggerates my tolerance for pain, but on this morning the tenderness throughout my body reminds me of what it truly means to be in agony. I could use a drink right now.

"This is why you don't help anyone," I grumble to myself. I curse myself for trying to help Rior – and all because he reminded me of my former squire, Laith. Look at the mess it got me into.

Still, he is just a boy, and my actions have put him in danger. It is only fair that I put it right. I hiss to myself as my moral compass kicks in yet again. I could do without it. This is the first time I have felt compelled to help anyone since I drank from that blasted fountain to protect my friends.

As I shuffle backwards against the cold stone, my eyes adjust to my dark surroundings. A beam of light trickles in from above just enough to tell me that I am in a prison cell, a slow, constant dripping noise its own form of torture. The smell is foul, even by my low standards. Shit, death, decay, and mould are the only things I can compare it to. I heave, barely managing to keep the limited contents of my stomach down.

What have I done to offend Morgana so much that she would strike me down in such a manner? Have we met before? Do I owe her a debt? Her magic was completely different from the flames I have seen Zerina wield, or even from the glamour that Esara cast to hide her true identity. This was something even more fierce, chaotic. I know I was stabbed during the fight in the markets, yet where my tunic is torn, no wound is present. She somehow moved my injuries to another, someone who is no longer of this earth. Why would she help me only to have me thrown into the dungeons?

"Rior." I speak his name out loud and panic overcomes me as I fear the fate he may have succumbed to in my absence. Will he think that I abandoned him? I hope for his sake that he has gone into hiding, somewhere safe from those Wyverns.

I search the dungeon for a way to escape, but the small opening where the light breaks in above me is too small for any person to climb through. I stagger towards the wrought-iron bars that block my exit and clasp hold of the metal. The coldness penetrates my skin, bringing a welcome reprieve from the pain. I shake the bars, testing them, but I am not surprised when they remain perfectly in place.

A bile rises in my throat, and the contents of my stomach eventually force their way out. The sting causes my eyes to stream and again I wonder what it is in the grand scheme of things to endure this miserable fate. Without realising it, a low grumble of frustration escapes my throat, and I cannot help but feel that the longer I am bearer of this curse, the more humanity I lose, and the more reptilian I become.

"Get back, beast!" a voice shouts, cutting through the sound of the dripping water.

An angered guard thrusts a pike towards me, and I stumble out of its trajectory just in time. I cannot blame him. I would be pissed off too if I had to work as a guard in this foul place. But my understanding only goes so far.

"What is it that I have done?" I hiss through the darkness, unsure if the guards can make out my hideous features or if they think I am just a man.

"I said get back!" The pike is pressed through the bars once more but this time I stand firm. The spiked end pushes against my thick skin. It causes me discomfort, but it does not pierce me, and I notice the look of surprise on the guard's face when he realises it has caused me no injury. He would need a lot more force than that if he wanted to harm me.

"Don't antagonise it!" a female guard scolds him. "Have you not heard of what it did down at the markets?"

It. I am no longer worthy of a name, apparently. I could not feel less human at this stage.

"I've heard Morgana is the one that should be feared," the male guard replies. "It isn't often that her magic is seen, but she certainly showed the Wyverns what it means to cross her path."

"Is that so?"

I recognise the voice as Morgana's, her steps becoming louder as the heels of her shoes echo off the stone floor. "I would say that it was a trip well taken then. Maybe these so-called Wyverns will see sense and heed my warning."

"Lady Morgana." The guards bow their heads, snapping to attention.

"Leave," she commands, and the two guards bow their heads once more before marching away down the corridor. No doubt to tease and goad another prisoner.

Morgana stands close enough to the bars to get a good look at me, but far enough away that I cannot reach her. Only one half of her face is revealed by the fragmented light.

"What brings you to Eltera, Orjan of Rashouya?" she asks, annunciating every syllable as she utters my name.

"Have I wronged you somehow?"

"Not yet."

For years I have not bothered anyone. I drink, I hide, I participate in the odd fight now and then. What could I have done to this woman?

I bow my head. "I was once Orjan of Rashouya." The shame of my former life presses to the forefront of my mind like a carriage racing down a hill without a horse, uncontrolled and unforgiving. How far I have come from leading the life of a knight. My sworn oaths broken, my boundaries knowing no limits. All because I succumb too easily to the lure of drink and gambling. Even when I thought I was building my life back in teaching young Laith the honour of a knight. Building a legacy.

"You managed quite the disappearing act," Morgana says. "Your whereabouts have been unknown for years, yet here you are. Bound and beaten in the dungeons of Eltera."

"Please, I need to return to the city. I have something I must attend to," I plead. I need to leave this place. Even if only to check that Rior is safe.

"Do you believe in the gods, Orjan?"

It is a simple enough question, yet I find it difficult to answer. "If there are gods, they know no bounds. Why else is it that they allow so much suffering in this world?"

"I believe that they exist. I believe the paths that we walk are fated, meticulously planned by the higher beings that watch over us, all-powerful. Why else would our paths cross?"

The idea that I am fated to live a cursed, miserable life doesn't comfort me in the slightest.

"I will allow you to leave to tend to your business, but you must in turn do something for me."

"Why would I do that?"

"Either stay in here and rot or do my bidding. You see, we have an issue in Eltera, one which you have already stumbled upon in the markets." Morgana runs her fingers across the bars. She is close enough for me to reach now, but killing her from inside this cell will not help me escape.

"The Wyverns."

"Yes, the Wyverns. They have become a big problem, yet their leader, Breyton, remains hidden. I want you to find him. End his control over the people of Eltera so that they can be properly governed." Morgana stares into my soul through the iron bars that divide us.

I meet her gaze. Though she tries to hide it, I can see that she is terrified of me, and I have no idea why, not when she possesses such power.

Morgana takes hold of my hand and closes her eyes. "This is a curious curse that you possess. I have never seen anything like it." She rubs her fingers over my scaled skin before placing the palms of her hands on the back of mine.

My skin stings as though sharp teeth pierce it. A green glow lights up our hands and grows brighter as if we clutch hold of a star, a soothing warmth replacing my pain with a comforting sensation. Sweat beads on Morgana's head as she focuses her magic, grimacing as if she is fighting to keep hold of my hand. When she lets go, I stare at my hand in shock. The scales that wrapped around my skin are gone, and my hand looks like it used to. I inspect my palm in disbelief, then excitedly feel my face. Disappointment quickly fills me when I realise that it is only my hand that is cured. When I bring my hand back down in front of me, my skin tone turns darker and the scales creep up from my wrist until no normal skin remains.

"No, no, no," I mutter in desperation. Years of searching for a cure have left me with nothing but broken hopes. This is the closest I have ever come to being free of this curse. "How – how did you do that?"

Morgana is panting heavily, her face riddled with discomfort. "My magic grows more powerful with every year that passes. Find Breyton and get me this city back, and I assure you I will do everything in my power to help rid you of that curse. Should you try to leave Eltera, I will have you tortured in ways that you cannot begin to imagine."

I nod reluctantly. If this is the only way I can rid myself of this ailment, then I must do her bidding. "You have my word."

"Let's hope your word means more than your reputation, Orjan." Morgana casts me an enchanting smile. "Find the leader of the Wyverns. Bring me Breyton's head."

But first, I must find Rior.

12

ORJAN

"The tale of the Borug-I is the tale of an Ork unlike any of his tribe, for this work was not a fan of murder and death, he was a bard and simply wished to bring joy to others. The Borug-I was shunned by his kind and exiled, as well as seen as a traitor to his people. He did not however change his ways and the ballad of Borug-I is often sang across the lands in raucous tune by those sinking ale and enjoying the company of friends."

The Borag-I, 115KR

RAIN LAPS against my skin with a force I am for once grateful to feel. The cold sensation reminds me that I am still alive somehow. Even better, the streets are empty as everyone seeks to remain sheltered in this torrential downpour, giving me freedom to move about the city unbothered.

Bring me Breyton's head. Morgana's request plays through my mind. This should not be too difficult, and it's a price I am willing to pay if Morgana's promises are true. But concern about Rior's wellbeing nags at me. If the Wyverns have hurt him in any way, I will show them the true meaning of pain.

It is the shelter where I head as I trudge through the thick mud created by this storm, the foul smell getting thicker and thicker the deeper into the slums I dive. So far, I have remained as close to the shadows as possible, and it is in my best intentions to remain this way.

When I reach the front of the shelter where Rior lives, the door is already ajar with little light inside. There is an eery quietness to this place, and my chest begins to thump against my tunic.

The door creaks as I make my way inside. My heart sinks. The shelter has been ransacked. The chairs at the sides of the room are broken, and chunks are missing from the walls where weapons and objects have been smashed against them. Judging by the looks of it, everything in this room has been destroyed. I can only hope that this is the worst it gets.

I step through the doorway into the kitchen area where I first came face-to-face with the Wyvern enforcer roughing up Rior. Here, pots and pans lay strewn across the work surfaces, and broken plates and cups are smashed into pieces across the floor. The wall rack hangs loosely, barely able to cling onto any form of stability. The pottery crunches under my feet as my breath quickens.

"Rior!" I call out. "Rior, it's Orjan."

Nothing but silence greets me. I continue my search of the kitchen to no avail. To the left of the room, I spot another doorway which opens to two sets of stairs, one leading upwards, one leading down into the cellar. My every judgement tells me not to head into the basement, but if I were a boy hiding, this is where I would go. I pluck a candle from the wall and light it using the flint that sits next to it, the warm glow offering a better view as I step into the darkness. I take the steps slowly as I descend, holding my breath.

"Rior?"

When I reach the basement, I see in an instant that it has also been ransacked. The Wyverns have already torn this place apart and I pray to the gods that they have not found Rior. The stores of grains have been destroyed, and it pains me to imagine how many will go hungry as a result. Wooden crates have also been broken into, chunks of wood missing where blades were used to pry their way in. The light from the candle causes a reflection and my stomach drops. Blood pools on the floor behind one of the crates. I walk towards the blood tentatively, unable to breathe, my heart feeling as though it may rip from my chest.

When I examine the body, I breathe a sigh of relief. It is not Rior, but Bravor who lies face down on the wet floor. The clothes on his back are soaked in crimson and his face is paler than the undead. Punctured marks shred his top. The man has not only been killed from behind, but whoever did this repeatedly stabbed him as though enraged. The man never stood a chance. I bow my head for a moment to pray for the man's kind soul. I can only hope that he greets a better afterlife than the misery he has suffered here.

A noise from the corner of the room cuts my respects short. Turning with the candle, I place my hand on my mace, assuming a defensive stance. A rat sits atop the seed, tucking its way into the banquet it has found. I shake my head and exhale, then gently carry Bravor's body upstairs before making my way to the top floor of the house. The stairs creak loudly as I ascend, and I fear what I may be about to walk into. One room to my right belongs to Rior's keepers – or at least, it did belong to them. A second room on the left contains a small bed that has been turned on its side. When I find no more bodies, I maintain some semblance of hope that the boy is still alive as I return to the main floor. If anything happened to him due to my actions, I am not sure I could endure the guilt. I have enough blood on my hands.

I hear movement behind me that is definitely not a rat, the creaking floorboard giving away their position. Before I have time to act, something smashes into my back, forcing me forwards into the wall. I feel nothing but a dull sensation against my armoured shell. I let out a low grumble to warn my attacker, and I turn to see a woman who stands in a state of shock. Her face is bloodied and her clothes are torn, relieving her of her modesty. Blood draws down her legs and I can only begin to think of the horrors this woman has had to endure.

"You bastard! You think you can just stroll back in here at Breyton's command!" Her voice cracks as she screams at me. "After everything your men have done to me!"

"Preya, it's me, Orjan!" I raise my hands to show I mean her no harm, but she keeps hold of her plank of wood, trembling. When she realises who I am, she lowers her weapon, her body and spirit shattered like glass.

"They killed him, they killed my husband. They raped me and murdered Bravor, I beg the gods to curse them for what they have done."

Had I not interfered with the enforcer, had I not broken his arm, had I not entered a fight and brawled with them in the streets of the markets, none of this would have happened. This is my fault. If not for me, this poor woman would still have her husband, her dignity.

"Preya, where is Rior?"

Preya screams in anger and drops to the sodden floor. I kneel in front of her and offer my hands to help her back up.

"I promise, I will make them pay for this. Please, is Rior okay?" The thought of something this severe happening to him fills me with a weighted dread in my stomach, and it catches me off guard. I haven't felt anything like this for so long, it reminds me that underneath my scaled skin, I am still human.

Preya's eyes stream with tears of stress, anger, and anguish, as she looks into my own before nodding her head lightly. "He is okay. I told him to hide, but I fear what he may have seen, what he may have heard. He is too young to witness all of this, he is just a boy!" Preya buries her head into my chest, her cries becoming muffled against my sodden tunic. I tentatively pat her back, unsure of how to comfort her.

"Orjan, Preya!" Rior emerges with a blanket in his hands, which he wraps around his keeper. His lip is bloodied and his clothes are torn, but aside from that, he appears somewhat okay.

Preya attempts to stand but her legs buckle and she falls back to her knees, knocking against the splintered floorboards. "Rior! You can't be here! If they find you, they will kill you." His presence seems to ignite a blind panic. "You need to leave! Bravor gave his life so you could escape. Go!"

Rior is stunned into silence, then he notices Bravor laid out on the floor behind me. Tears fill his eyes. "They killed Bravor?" He collapses to his knees and Preya wraps her arms around him as he weeps for his fallen keeper. "It's all my fault," the boy sobs uncontrollably, his chest heaving as though he is about to be sick, as if he struggles to breathe. It is a level of grief he has likely not endured before, neither should he at his young age. "Had I not gone to the markets, that fight would never have broken out."

My heart drops like a stone thrown down a deep well for

how this day has forged this boy's fate. His life is in ruins, his keeper is dead, and his safety is compromised. Worse still, Rior blames himself, when in truth, I am to blame for this mess. The situation is even worse than when I abandoned Laith. Everything I touch turns to ashes. It is I that is the curse that plagues these lands. Sorrow and scorn shadow me wherever I go.

I need to right this wrong. I need to maintain this boy's safety. Suddenly, bringing Morgana Breyton's head feels like a privilege instead of a chore.

"The Wyverns, Breyton, where do I find them?" I ask, my blood boiling with rage.

"No one knows who Breyton is," says Preya through strained tears. "But at nighttime, the Wyverns meet by the old library. They hold arranged fights there. Offer people the chance of food and coin as a reward for taking part. All so they can keep themselves entertained."

"You two need to stay hidden until I return to tell you it's safe."

"Where are you going?" Rior asks.

"I think it's time I went to pay these Wyverns a visit."

13

MORGANA

"**Y**ou mean to tell me that this man has taken over your kingdom and you have no information on him whatsoever?"

Wistler squirms in his seat as the two of us dine, our conversation proving fruitless.

"I have tried, Morgana. No one will answer the questions I ask." Wistler sips his wine, swilling it around his mouth.

"Then you need to make them answer," I seethe. "You must be willing to apply the necessary pressure in order to bend people to your will. It is a method which I have become particularly skilled at. Getting others to do as I wish."

Wistler's eyes widen as I bring a piece of carrot to my mouth and begin to chew it slowly. He gulps down his wine as though settling his nerves. "Pressure does not work with the Wyverns. I am trying to gather information so that I can bring them down from the inside."

"Three years you have tried this approach, to no avail. For three years you have allowed these vermin to control one of the most crucial forges of Levanthria, thus failing to provide your king with the armour his army requires. Athos is most displeased."

"I'm not the one who freed a dangerous beast to freely roam the streets. I don't understand how letting a monster loose in the kingdom will bring people to heel."

"Sending in this monster means that blood can be shed without the common people of these lands blaming us. They will grow to fear Orjan and what he is capable of, the chaos he will bring." I smile as I reach for my cup and take my own sip of wine.

Wistler narrows his eyes. "What good will that do us?"

"When he has done our bidding and lain waste to the Wyverns, the people of Eltera will see us defeat him and they will thank us for putting an end to his terror. They will gaze upon us with gratitude and loyalty."

"And that will bring the people back under my rule?" Wistler asks.

"Of course. You'll be their hero, Wistler." I cringe inwardly at the words, but Wistler's face lights up. I have no doubt that if it came to actually taking a life, Wistler would have someone else do it for him and then take the credit. The man has no honour.

"Excellent." He rubs his hands together in anticipation of the plan bearing its fruits. "In the meantime, I will have my messengers communicate with my spies to grant aid to this monster when they can."

"It is in your best interest that Orjan succeeds in his task, Wistler," I tell him. "The king's resources grow lower with every passing day. It is crucial that we resupply his forces with ironite armour." The king might need the forge to restock his armour, but I have other plans for it once we reclaim it from the Wyverns.

Wistler raises his cup towards me. "Well, here is to the end of the Wyverns. To Eltera."

"To all of Levanthria." I tap my cup against his before taking another sip of wine, an explosion of flavour filling my mouth. I can't help but smile. As long as I know where Orjan is and that he is alive, I see no reason for my vision to come true. Laith will have no reason to strike me down to avenge his former master if Orjan is alive and well.

"Tell me, Morgana, what is it that drives you to serve the king in such a way? Is it riches for yourself? To leave a legacy for your family name?"

"I have no family, not anymore." I speak the words sharply, without thinking. I regret it instantly. Information is power, and now I've just handed over personal information to this snivelling man.

A flurry of motion catches my attention from the doorway as one of the guards steps towards us. She removes a dagger from her side, and before I can react, she launches it in our direction. It barely misses my face as I feel the force of air against my cheek. The woman's eyes widen when she realises that she missed her target. I feel my face contort with rage at the insolence of her pathetic assassination attempt.

Wistler dives under the table to protect himself. "Guards!" he cries out.

Another sentry lunges at our would-be assassin and attempts to hold her, but the nimble woman evades him. In one swift motion, she unsheathes her sword and plunges it through the man's stomach. He splutters blood from his mouth before dropping to the floor to take his final breaths.

The assassin swirls to enter combat with the two new guards that burst into the room. Her skill with a blade astounds me and the men are no match for her. I make my way towards her as she continues to dance around the guards, dodging and parrying their strikes as she attempts to flee. She drives her blade into the face of one before spinning and slicing across the stomach of the other, then meets my eyes. I see panic there. Undoubtedly, she knows that harsh punishment awaits her for her treason.

My temper flares, and I fight to keep control as a surge of energy rises within me. The tingling sensation increases until the pressure becomes too much. As I release my magic, the assassin dives out of the way, and my power sends a suit of armour crashing to the floor, melting a hole through the metal.

The assassin looks from me to the door, calculating. Then she sets off at a sprint, putting distance between us at speed despite the armour she wears. I concentrate my magic and feel a ripple of euphoric power travel through me like fresh cold water running over my skin. The woman is fast, but I have learnt how to harness my magic to improve my speed. Within seconds I am at her heel, and when she shoots a glance over her shoulder, she is shocked by my proximity. This is her biggest mistake. If she had remained focused, she may have just been able to make it out of the castle alive.

With a burst of energy, I dive towards the assassin and catch her legs, sending us both crashing to the ground. Pain sears through my limbs as magic and rage consume me. I roll the assassin onto her back, but she strikes me in the face, angering me even further. It has been some time since I had a good old-fashioned brawl. I feel alive with fury as I strike a blow down on the woman, landing another and another. Her face erupts into a bloodied mess, her nose crooked and broken and her eyes swelled. I raise my hand for a final blow, but I stop myself, taking a breath, and the assassin groans weakly before slipping into unconsciousness. I smile at her, spitting my own blood onto her chest plate.

My body trembles with the aftereffects of magic use. By now, the life force I absorbed from the Wyvern in the market has worn off, and I've drawn upon my own stores. I embrace the feeling rather than fear it, allowing the sensation to consume me as it sends an icy chill down my spine, causing me to shudder. In this moment, I care not that an assassin or spy has somehow found their way into the castle. What I care for is to reclaim some life force from this person to compensate for the magic I have used.

Then, I shall drag this woman deep into the dungeon and extract as much information from her as I can before she takes her final breaths.

14

ORJAN

"Jonah Viergen claims to be the master of knowledge around the ironite yet so far he has been unable to help me with my theories. Maybe I need to tend to him in a manner that is more persuasive, it is amazing how the mind can think of when certain pressures are applied. To the body and to those that are closest to them."

Diary entry of Morgana, 253KR

THE DARKNESS GRANTS me reprieve as I traverse the outer walls to the southern gate of Eltera, towards the old library. The night brings with it a coldness that causes my breath to fog, as if I hold fire in my belly. And indeed, I feel the flames of anger growing within me. I have no idea what I am going to do when I meet the Wyverns. All I know is that I must find a way to ensure that Rior and Preya do not live in fear for their lives from this Breyton's sick notion of justice.

Raucous laughter and cheers ring out as a crowd of rowdy men and woman stumble from outside a large building lit from within. It is a circular building with a large dome at the top made from the finest of stone. It looks like I've found the old library – and the Wyverns.

Thin, elongated windows form a symmetrical line around the perimeter of the building, filled with pristine stained glass. Each one depicts different tales and history of Levanthria. Within the glass of one I see the tale of the famed monster hunter, Gregor Yerald, the colourful artwork depicting the dybukk that he heroically rid a village of. I am amazed that these windows have remained in place given the state of disrepair that the rest of the kingdom lies in.

As I move towards the crowd, hushed whispers begin to form. My scarf hides my face, but my height is impossible to ignore.

"That's him, from the market!"

"Breyton has put a price on his head,"

"Look at the size of him."

"I heard he ripped a man's arm off."

I tut at the exaggerations. It was Morgana who truly brought gore to the fight, with her magic laying waste to anyone that stood against us. I hold the gaze of one of the men who speaks, and he shrinks away, ushering the others to follow him.

When I reach the entrance to the library, a wave of smoke and ale accost my senses, my ears filled with the cheering from a noisy crowd baying for blood. I force my way through the thick throng of people to find what it is everyone is cheering for.

The ground has been dug out to form a large pit. Around its top outer edge, spectators spill over the sides of a large wooden rail, waving their hands furiously at the two men brawling below. One stands slightly larger than the other, giving him an edge over his adversary. He straddles the smaller fighter, raining down punches on his head and face, each crunching blow piercing the sound of the cheering crowd. The audience roars as the victor delivers one final punch before standing tall. It is unclear whether his opponent is dead or breathing, but his face is unrecognisable. The thickset man has not come out of this fight unharmed, though. He carries a limp and smarts from his own injuries, although and I can't tell if the blood belongs to him or the man who lies broken in the dirt.

Applause rings out, and the man stretches his arms out in appreciation of their support. Men and women clamber down some steps to drag the beaten man's body out and away. The winner of the fight follows up the steps where he is greeted by a man in fine silks. My stomach gives a jolt. Is this the man I am searching for? Is this the man that could lead to my freedom from this curse?

"We have our winner, Maru!" the newcomer shouts. His fineries make him stand out from the rest of the crowd, and his words are well-spoken, meaning he may be highborn. His short white hair is slicked back, and his face wears the marks of time, the one thing we are all limited to. And if this is Breyton, his time is limited indeed.

The crowd cheers loudly again, and the man raises Maru's arm before passing him a single coin. All that effort, all that pain, for one coin? These people must be desperate. Maru nods in appreciation and makes to leave.

"Are you ready for the next fight?" the man in silks calls out, and the crowd cheers again. Next, two women descend the steps into the pit. The woman on the right has long blond hair tied back, her clothes ragged and torn. She doesn't look like a fighter, and the colour drains from her face as the crowd roars. Her opponent on the left carries toned muscles and her hair is cut short, a tactic employed by seasoned fighters as it gives opponents less to grab hold of.

She stands stony-faced, her muscles tensed as she jabs into the air, her eyes fixed on her weaker opponent. Her eyes are wild with the excitement from the pit. No sooner does the fight start, the short-haired woman runs towards the nervous blonde and yanks her by the ponytail before landing a sickening punch to her face. As the crowd cheers on, it is clear to me what the outcome of this mismatched fight will be.

Having seen enough, I head to the far side of the pit in search of the old man dressed in fine silks. My hand shakes with rage, but I gather myself as best I can. If I am to get close enough to their leader to take his head, I will need to appear approachable, despite wanting to tear his throat out for what he did to Bravor, for what his men did to Preya.

I find him sitting at a table with three men wearing matching dark leather-bound tunics. When they see me, their conversation stops, and the three thugs stand up as if protecting their elder.

"I seek merely to talk," I lie.

"You caused a lot of damage in the markets." The man's voice cuts past his enforcers, causing them to stop in their tracks. "Tell me, what gives you the audacity to come to my fighting pit after slaughtering my people as though they were dogs?"

"They attacked first."

"Our messengers tell us that you have interfered with our business on two separate occasions."

"On both occasions, your business involved roughing up a defenceless child."

"I assume you are already aware of the consequences your actions have brought."

My temper flares at the calmness in his callous words. "You slaughtered his keeper, beat and raped his wife."

"I merely acted on the commands of Breyton when I told our men to do what they saw fit to avenge their fallen brothers and sisters."

So, this man isn't Breyton – but then, who is he?

The man looks disinterested in our conversation. "Now if you don't mind, we have coin to collect from these fights. If not for my concern for the bloodshed of my men, I would have you brought to your knees right here, in front of everyone."

I would like to see them try.

"Stay away from Rior and Preya," I warn. I may have failed with Laith, Zerina, and Esara, but I refuse to repeat the same mistakes with Rior and Preya. I will do what I must to right this wrong. It is the only way I can maintain any semblance of a soul.

"And tell me, why would we do that? We will stop only when we have seen to it that justice is served."

"Yet it was I that committed the crimes." Reluctantly, I bite down the temptation to end this man's life here and now. I might need him if I am to find Breyton.

"And it was he and his keepers that avoided paying our men when we came to collect." He smiles and takes a drink of the ale that sits in front of him. One of the men raises his hand to the hilt of his blade, flashing me a cocksure smile. Another stares at me darkly, his smile sinister and goading. One thing is for sure, his men are ready for a fight, maybe some revenge for what I did to the others in the markets.

"You will leave them alone or I will find Breyton and I will kill him."

"Do you think you are the first to make threats towards him?" The man becomes lost in his thoughts for a moment. "I will tell my men to leave them alone, but I want something in return." His smile is more like a snarl. "After all, if it is not something that will benefit the Wyverns, they will carry out their task and most likely kill this child that you clearly hold dear."

I curse myself for coming here without a plan. "What is it you ask?"

"You will fight. Someone new in the pit will keep spirits lifted and the coffers full."

It seems simple enough to me. Win a fight, and Rior and Preya will remain safe. "Fine," I answer. "Promise you will not harm the boy or his keeper, and I will engage in a fight for you."

"No, no, no." He waves his finger from side to side, shaking his head. "Fights. If I agree to your terms, you will fight until I deem you surplus, unless the pit brings your downfall before then."

The man's demands are high and the last thing I want is to become a spectacle for the bloodthirsty audience. But if I play along, perhaps I can gain further information on Breyton, and end all this.

"Tell me, do we have a deal?" The man offers his hand.

"We have a deal," I answer, but I do not take his offer of a handshake.

"Very well, the boy's safety is guaranteed, providing you uphold your end. What is your name, so I can announce you?"

"Orjan," I answer. "And you?" I should at least know the name of the man I do business with.

"My name is Trovell. Well, Orjan shall we get straight to it?"

"Now?"

"Or I could pay your little friend a visit." Trovell walks past me and heads towards the pit. Following him, I see that the fight with the two women has drawn to an end. The inexperienced fighter is a crumpled mess in the corner, her body battered.

"We have another winner," Trovell calls out as the cheering crowd salutes the woman. "As promised, the winner will receive just rewards."

The short-haired fighter walks up the steps towards Trovell and places her hand out. Trovell drops a single coin into her palm, and she clasps her hand shut before walking off. As she walks off, she bumps her shoulder into Trovell's, shoving past him. Trovell appears flustered momentarily by this subtle act of rebellion, but quickly focuses his attention back on the fighter who remains sprawled in the pit.

"It is not just those who win that gain payment," Trovell explains to me. "Those brave enough to fight in the pit will also receive a food parcel for their efforts."

Below, the loser is heaved to her feet by some stewards who drag her up the steps. "Have her taken to the healers," Trovell commands. "She will need to fight again to repay that debt to us." He smirks, and a heat of anger rises in me. I have fallen ill of this kind of debt in the past. Such a debt becomes nigh impossible to repay, and so the spiral will start. Once again, I contemplate ripping Trovell's head from his shoulders in front of everyone, but I must suppress this temper. It would only put Rior in more danger.

Trovell raises his hands and the crowd falls silent. "Are you ready for one final fight?"

The crowd roars, clearly not finished with the spilling of blood in this once hallowed building.

"Some of you may have seen this man as he brawled in the streets. We have him here to fight any person who wishes to challenge him. I will pay three, no five coins to anyone who can best him."

A wave of apprehension seems to replace the crowd's raucous chants as eyes turn towards me.

I take the steps down into the pit where the smell of blood mixed with dirt engulfs my senses. Hushed anticipation soon turns to heckling, and I try to block out the jeers of the crowd.

"I'll take that coin!" A broad, bare-chested man follows me into the pit, and the crowd applauds him with wild enthusiasm.

He laughs, then lunges straight for me. I step forward to meet him, launching a fierce punch. His momentum is his undoing as his face meets my fist with a crunch. He slams to the ground before starting to convulse, and the crowd falls silent in an instant.

Stewards run down to tend to the man as the crowd's jeers and boos grow louder once more, unimpressed with the outcome of the fight. It is all empty noise to me, I have no need for them to cheer my name.

All I want is Breyton.

15

ORJAN

Trovell stands over the pit as if he has just found gold, his wide smile and sunken eyes watching over as the man who stood against me continues to convulse from my blow.

Two men and a woman drop into the pit, their fists already bound. One of the men already has bruises purpling his face. This is not their first fight of the night.

"Three against one." Trovell grins. "Who here likes those odds?" The crowd bays, and a flurry of hands above us begin to exchange coins on who will win this fight.

I keep my back to the wall so that they cannot surround me, at least for now. The trio edges towards me, confident in their numbers like a wild pack of animals. My strength is far superior to theirs, but the thought that they may just be entering the pits in order to provide for their families enters my mind. In this moment, I make a conscious decision not to use my full strength on them. Little do they know that even with three against one, the odds are stacked greatly against them.

The smaller man on the right appears somewhat hesitant to strike and it is through him I will counter. The man in the centre nods to the others and lunges forward, but the three of them are out of sync. I feign a jab with my left towards the smallest man and he flinches, leaving the larger man in the middle exposed. I step into the space and swing my left arm once more. This time my fist meets with the larger man's jaw with a sickening thud. Blood spills from his mouth and sprays over the woman who seems somewhat invigorated by it, almost bathing in it. She strikes me across the face, nearly knocking my scarf down. I glance at her before bringing my forearm around which connects with her side, knocking her backwards. The third opponent makes his move, but it is a cowardly strike; he swings at me whilst my attention is on another. More fool him. As I turn away, he meets the hardened shell on my back. I feel only a dull thud, but the man's cries of pain bring shocked cheers from the crowd who continue to roar on the fight. I turn to face the coward and find that his hand flaps around loosely, his wrist clearly broken. In his panic he attempts to strike me with his other hand, but I grab hold of his arm with ease, warding off his feeble attempt to strike me. He shrinks into himself as panic overcomes him. I take pity on the man, and forcibly push him away from me. As he stumbles, the other two fighters have become more synchronised. They move towards me at the same time, throwing a flurry of blows against my body as I tuck my arms in to protect myself.

The crowd continues to chant loudly with every blow that lands but in truth, none of the blows cause me much difficulty. Counting the blows against me, I bide my time as I figure out the fighting styles they are using. Then, as the female fighter aims another blow, I grab hold of her, guarding myself with my free arm. I pull her towards me before crashing my shoulder into her. She falls backwards but I do not relent. I pull her towards me again, landing another crunching blow, but I'm holding back, trying to restrain my strength. She stumbles backwards and I let go as the biggest of the three rakes his hand down my face, displacing my scarf. Large gasps escape the crowd as they are introduced to my cursed face for the first time.

"Monster."

"He's hideous."

"Animal."

I try to drown out the insults they hurl at me. Their words are no different from what I have used to describe myself. However, having this many people scream abuse at me at once, in tandem, brings a whole new level of shame that weighs me down like a boulder. A knot forms in my back as I look away from the crowd, staring into the floor as they continue to hurl abuse at me as if I am the lowest of criminals. Something small and hard hits me in the back of the head, followed by the sound of shattering glass, and I realise the crowd has begun throwing stones, tankards, and bottles at me. My skin is thick enough to protect me from physical assaults, but the words they use to insult me cuts deeper than any blade could.

I am a monster in their eyes, a hideous abomination cast down by the gods. A curse on anyone who tries to aid me.

Horrified by my appearance, the large man steps away from me. He glances to his right at a broken bottle that sits by his feet and leans down to pick it up in desperation.

"I wouldn't do that," I growl. Items from the crowd continue to ricochet off me.

The man makes his choice and lunges for me. I jump backwards, avoiding the strike, and he swings again, then a third time. The fourth blow connects with my arm, and I wince at the burning sensation that engulfs my bicep. The pain brings me back to this world from my fleeting thoughts, anger rising up within me like the plumes of a volcano before it erupts. The cut doesn't feel too deep, but it is enough to bring me discomfort and increase my frustration. The man foolishly attempts to strike me again, but I land a blow to his midriff. He stops in his tracks, instantly winded, and I seize my opportunity to take hold of the broken bottle in his hand.

"I told you not to do that!" My words almost hiss as I scold the man. His strength does not match my own, and I smash my fist into the inner bicep of the arm holding the bottle. As his arm goes limp, I redirect his hand and the bottle towards his own head. The bottle disintegrates as it makes contact with his skull, and the man staggers back. I rush into his space once more and plant both my fists into his chest with enough force to cause serious injury, my anger getting the better of me. Surely the fool knows he cannot beat me. If these people want to see a monster, then I will show them a monster.

I roar as I strike once more. His ribs crack and snap from the blow, and the man is lifted clean off the ground before landing on the bed of glass that surrounds us.

The smallest man scurries towards the steps, having had enough of the flight. An unwise choice, as now his back is turned to me. I launch myself on him, sending him sliding through the glass and dirt, and he screams in pain as his skin tears underneath us. Straddling him from behind, I grab a fist full of his hair and arch his back towards me as I hiss in his ear. "A monster, am I!"

"I – I didn't say you were," the man pleads.

I smash his head into the ground, rendering him unconscious with a ferociously feral force, snarling like every inch of the beast they wish to see, instinct taking control of me.

The woman and this man lie unconscious, and the largest groans loudly as he writhes around in pain in the dirt, the broken glass crunching underneath him.

"He's an animal!" one voice calls.

"He's a dragon!" another announces.

"Dragon, Dragon, Dragon!"

Some of the crowd begins to chant their new name for me, but the majority continues to hurl insults at me, some even going so far as to spit on me. In this moment, I despise the Wyverns for making me hurt these people. Although I tried to hold back, I am sure their broken and bruised bodies will not feel that way in the morning. At least I can take solace in the fact that Breyton's thugs will leave Rior and Preya alone.

I look up at the group of men and woman surrounding the pit, their faces contorting with rage towards me. They hate me, yet they do not know me. If only they knew that their hatred pales in comparison to what I feel for myself.

As I climb the stairs out of the pit, broken glass crunches under my boots. The stale taste of ale hangs on my breath, a dull headache beginning to set in.

Trovell waits for me at the top of the stairs with a hulking thug on either side of him.

"Where do you think you are going?" he sneers. "We are not done yet."

The balding brute to his left grins and plants his boot into my chest, catching me off guard. The force causes the air to escape my lungs, winding me. As I fall backwards, the room spins around me, and I bounce back down the steps into the centre of the pit. Glasses and bottles smash around me. One man even empties his bladder into the pit, and the crowd roars with laughter. I stare at the ground, trying not to react.

Placing my knuckles into the floor, I push myself upwards, standing as tall as my encased back will allow me to.

16

MORGANA

"There are those who believe that all magic hails from Elven heritage, meaning to wield magic you must be from a direct bloodline. No matter how diluted, the power of magic can be unlocked. They are however considered fanatics of a forgotten age. And so the band of Elorash and their banners are exiled from society, their membership only revealed by a tattoo of an eye, believed to represent their god of power Rayandregor. They believe that one day, he will return to the lands that humans walk and unlock the power of magic within all those who hold the once great bloodline."

Reitu Tvesh, The Codex Of Elorash, 186KR

THE QUALITY of torture implements I have on hand are disappointing, far from the collection that I have amassed in the dungeons of Askela. The black, rough stone walls shine as dampness clings to them, a yellowish green moss cultivating on its surface.

I inhale deeply to focus my mind and reach down to the bucket of water by my side, emptying the stagnant water over the bound woman's head. She is hoisted into the air by her arms, her head stooped forward, still unconscious. Congealed blood trails from her mouth, her shoulders looking displaced by the weight they are bearing. The water splashes over her, soaking her to her skin, and she begins to murmur, slowly lifting her head up until her amber eyes meet my own.

"What do you want with me?" Her voice is taut with pain, and her accent is like what I have become accustomed to from the locals. There is a roughness to her words, as though she has swallowed glass. Now there is some food for thought. Maybe dining on some glass will teach her for her cowardly assassination attempt.

"Who is it that sent you?"

The woman stares me in the eyes before pulling her head back, then spits at me. Thick mucus mixed with blood splashes against my face. My temperature soars and I grab hold of the woman's wrist with gritted teeth and squeeze. I focus some of my power to my hand, and soon her skin begins to crack and sizzle. The smell of her singed flesh flares my nostrils. It is a repugnant smell that I am still not used to.

The woman screams, flailing wildly where she hangs. I make sure I keep eye contact with her as her wails echo throughout the chamber. She will pay for her insubordination.

After a few agonising moments, I let go of her arm, and her eyes are drawn to the blackened skin around her wrist.

"Test me again, and I will remove your eyes." I wipe her blood from my face with the sleeve of my dress. Her face is already swollen and bruised from her beating, but I would love nothing more than to add to her list of ailments.

"Are you sorry?" I ask.

The woman smiles at me and doesn't answer. I strike her across her face with an open hand. The familiar crackling noise of skin burning starts to escape from under my hand, but this is quickly eclipsed as she screams far louder this time.

"Stop, stop!" she cries, tears cascading down her face. I remove my hand and the droplets turn to vapour as they reach her torched cheek.

"Are you sorry for spitting at me?"

"I am," she mumbles.

"I didn't quite hear that." I stretch out my fingers in front of her face before moving to grab her arm.

"I'm sorry, please just keep your hands away from me." She winces as I move my hand away. At least I have her cooperation now. Even by my standards this one has broken far easier than I imagined.

I raise my hand gently to her face, and she flinches under my touch, her breathing becoming shallow and quickened. I wipe away the tears on her cheek with my thumb and lean in towards her. "Who was it that sent you to kill me?"

"I can't – I can't tell you. They will kill my family," the woman answers in a panicked state. She fears me, but she seems to fear her employers more.

"Have you not learned your lesson?" I yank her hair back, snapping her neck away from me. She strains against me, so I clench my fist harder, tightening my grip on her hair. "You have no idea the depths of depravity I will go for the answers that I want. You have seen what I can do with magic, but you would be equally terrified if you saw first-hand what I can do with tools."

"Please, don't." Her voice quivers as I cast my eyes over the small table besides us. I reach for a dagger and stare at the blade for a moment before wrapping the palm of my free hand around it. I take a sharp intake of breath before I begin to squeeze the blade tightly. My skin tears and the sensation feels soothing for a moment before a sharp stinging pain engulfs my hand. I linger on the pain for a moment, savouring the throbbing feeling. Blood escapes through my fingertips, and for a moment I get lost, staring at my blood as it drips onto the cold stone floor.

Closing my eyes, I channel my magic. A dark, eery glow emits from my closed fist. I look at the prisoner and begin to murmur an incantation under my breath. This is one that I have near perfected over the last year. Slowly the throbbing sensation subsides, and I release the knife. My blood remains, but my wound is gone.

The woman begins to scream as the cut is transferred to her. She jerks wildly, confused by what is happening. As she looks up towards her bound wrist, thick, crimson blood begins to trail down her arm. "What witchcraft is this?" She shakes her hands as if to break free of her chains.

"Do I look as though I am here casting curses and boiling brews in a cauldron? I am a sorceress, not a witch. A spell caster unrivalled by any man that walks this world. Now, who was it that sent you?"

"Please, I didn't want to." She continues to writhe, suspended in the air. "I didn't have a choice. They told me that if I assassinated you, they would absolve all my debts, that me and my family would be free. My husband wouldn't need to fight in the pits anymore."

"The pits?"

"It's where they get people to fight for money, a way of entertaining people but also giving others the opportunity to win rations and coin."

"And who is they?"

"You already know."

I step towards her and slice her arm with the dagger, a light laceration becoming visible through her torn tunic.

"Please, stop!"

I add three more cuts, two to her arm and one to her stomach.

"The Wyverns!" she finally cries out. "It was the Wyverns that sent me. Breyton wants you dead."

I smile. So, I have already gotten his attention.

"Was it worth it?" I tease. "Was it worth all this pain for what you were promised?"

"It was either that or we starve, while watching my husband lose all his dignity in the pits."

I consider my prisoner, pondering her words. "I can make all your pain go away," I tell her. "I can make your debts disappear, too. And I will give you fresh coin to leave Eltera and start a new life."

The woman furrows her brows. "What is it you ask of me in return?" she asks, her voice quivering.

"You will tell me everything that is going on with the Wyverns. If you deceive me, however, you, your husband, and your children will all suffer a fate far worse than what I have introduced you to today. Do you understand?"

The woman nods. "I'll do it."

"What is your name?"

"Delaya."

"Now, my little sparrow, the first thing I need you to do is report back on what Orjan is up to. He is a man I already have on the inside. You will know who I mean. He doesn't exactly blend in."

"I know of who you speak."

"Let him know he has an ally in you, but do not let it be

known it is I who sent you." After all, I do not know the beast's true allegiance. It will be good to have eyes on him, just in case.

17

ORJAN

I stare into the fire in an empty room, the flames of which lick my sodden clothes. Shame washes over me for my actions in the pit, but I did what I had to do to secure Rior's safety. Now I take a large gulp of the spirit clutched in my hand. It burns my throat as I drink it in, but for each gulp I take, the shame I feel lessens.

The door behind me creaks open and I can't help but prepare myself to fight once more. It is Trovell, his aged, pointed face engraved with a crooked smile. He enters the room accompanied by one of his thugs, his nose lifted as though greeted by an offensive smell.

"Well, well, well," Trovell starts, "you have put on quite the show."

I grip the neck of the bottle tightly in my hand as the urge to smash it across his smug face nearly consumes me. It is only the thoughts of the consequences for Rior that prevent me from following through with the temptation.

"Will you honour your word?" I ask.

"The boy and his keeper will see no harm from the Wyverns. For now." His grin widens.

I take a step towards him, fist clenched, but his thug steps in front of him, blocking my path.

"Now, now, Dragon." Trovell waves a finger at me. "That is precisely the kind of reaction that will get the boy you seek to protect an early meeting with the afterlife."

I grit my teeth. "Do not call me that."

"My men will call you whatever they see fit," Trovell sneers. "This is Grush, by the way. He will be keeping tabs on you. I suggest you follow his direction."

I stare the two of them down. It's one thing to be bested by someone better than you in combat. It is another to manipulate someone to do your bidding, the ultimate cowardice.

"Grush has some errands to run for me. When I speak with him tomorrow, I had best hear of nothing other than compliance. Do you understand, Dragon?"

My muscles tense and the bottle that I grasp shatters. Some of the contents spray into the fireplace, igniting the flames.

"Come on," Grush says, "we have much to do." Grush stops in front of me and looks me up and down. "Take off your scarf, I want people to see you for what you are. Hideous."

I stare into his unflinching eyes, my jaw clenched tightly. I hide my face behind my scarf so that I don't have to deal with the gasps of people when they see my face.

"Is there a problem?" he asks me, all the while puffing his chest out as if he hopes to intimidate me.

Raising my hand to my face, I lower my scarf and glower at the brute. "Just remember that it is only circumstance that binds my hands behind my back," I growl. "If that was to change –"

"Is that a threat?" Grush enters my space and stands

nose-to-nose with me. He is a giant of a man and his putrid breath offends me.

"I seek only to let you know that for now, my hands are tied."

"Don't be getting into a brawl before we have even started," Trovell scolds as he pulls a cloak over his shoulders, rolling his eyes at the two of us.

Trovell heads off towards what I presume are his chambers whilst I follow Grush out into the streets of Eltera.

It is the dead of night, the air is still, and there is little noise other than the last of the drunkards making their way home.

"This way, Dragon."

I stand still.

"Dragon, you heard Trovell. If I report back that you haven't followed every single order that I have given you, your little rat friend will meet a grim end. Stop acting so fucking virtuous all the time." He sets off down the street. "This way, you ugly bastard."

He struts down the street like a prized horse. I follow him reluctantly, keeping myself a few paces behind to avoid the temptation to smash his head into the dirt. I find myself stumbling as the alcohol seeps into my system. Looking up at the night sky, I see there is no moon in sight, with only the stars offering sparkling light from above.

We carry on for a few streets before Grush eventually stops outside a house that looks as if it has seen better days. I wonder what he would want with such a building or why he would be here.

"Kick the door in," he says.

I hesitate, but there are worse things that he could be asking me to do than break into what looks like an empty, derelict building. I move in front of the door and plant a full boot just below the handle. The door splinters as it is ripped from its hinges from the force.

I instantly regret it when children's screams ring out from the darkness within.

"What in the blazes!" A full-bearded man even larger than Grush stands before us, a night shirt covering his modesty. His wife joins his side, and her eyes widen as she takes in the monster that stands before them. She screams, staggering back, and Grush rushes past me. In this moment it is clear why Grush had me remove my scarf, he wants people to fear the monster that was hidden underneath. He wants me to be the monster that he sees, what they all see.

"Keep that whore wife of yours under control, Heath!"

Heath turns to his wife. "Go and sit with the children. Stay in there, no matter what you hear."

She does as she is told. Heath's eyes follow her until the door creaks shut. He then trails his eyes to stare down at the two of us. "What is it you want?"

Grush plucks an apple off the kitchen table and inspects it. "I heard a rumour, Heath, that you are involved in a little group. One that intends to overthrow the Wyverns." He takes a bite of the apple whilst leaning against the table. "You've hurt Breyton's feelings."

"You people make me sick," Heath says. "There is no honour about you. You rule this place with fear, for your own gain. You mention Breyton but no one has met this man. We seek only to make our kingdom prosper, for the people of Eltera to be able to make a good, honest living." He stands defiantly, unintimidated by Grush's smaller stature.

"So, you admit your contempt?"

Heath clenches his fists. "I admit nothing, this is a fool's court!"

"Careful, Heath, you would not want to antagonise this situation." Grush seems to relish every moment, chewing his apple.

"Antagonise!" Heath roars. "You come here in the dead of night and kick my door through, take fruit from my table. In front my children, my wife!" He lunges for Grush, and the two clash together as Grush bowls over the table with Heath on top of him. As they crash to the floor, the table falls over beside them, sending the fruit across the room. An orange rolls to my foot as I watch Heath throw punches at Grush.

Grush grins wildly, savouring every blow that is rained down on him. Then he throws Heath to his side and stands, dusting himself off before offering Heath another chance to fight him.

Heath attempts to spear him again, but this time Grush is unmoving when Heath dives into him. He drops his elbow onto Heath's back over and over again until he pushes himself away. Without hesitation, Heath throws another punch, but Grush blocks him before volleying his own blow. Heath's nose explodes and his head snaps back. He drops to his knees whilst Grush takes hold of his hair and pulls his head backwards, landing another strike. Heath slumps to the floor, bordering unconsciousness.

"Well, don't think you will just be standing there." Grush looks at me, then grabs Heath's ankle and drags him to the table. He places his leg over the leg of the table before standing up and dusting himself off.

"Break it," he demands.

"Break what?"

"The table," he answers sarcastically. "His fucking leg! Break it."

This man may have wronged the Wyverns somehow, but

he has not wronged me. "You have bested him, Grush. What honour is there in maiming him further?"

Grush's face reddens. "It has nothing to do with honour, Dragon! We need to send a message. Now, break his leg!"

As I step towards Heath, he mumbles words under his swollen face, spitting blood over himself in the process.

"Please don't do this."

I hesitate, but I know what will happen to Rior if I do not follow Grush's order. At least Heath will keep his life. Rior probably won't be afforded the same privilege.

I stamp down on Heath's shin and a sickening crack is followed by his scream of pain.

"There's a good little dog!"

I feel sickened by my actions, and I look away.

Grush kneels by Heath's head. "If I hear you're meeting with others about any form of revolt, it will be your family that we come back for." He slams Heath's head into the floor where he slips into unconsciousness.

"Let this be a lesson to them. Let them know of the dragon who will come in the night!" Grush grins. "Come, Dragon,"

"Where are we going now?"

"We have another couple of visits before we call it a night."

I deplore this man, who seems to savour the pain that he gives out to the people of Eltera, a pain that I am forced to be complicit with. All at the command of a man that no one seems to have seen, a man who holds all the power to this city.

I have to put an end to this.

18

MORGANA

"*Magic once outlawed is now sought to be brought under control in order to win the King's war against the Zarubian empire. King Athos Almerion overruled ancient degree lasting hundreds of years as he realised that countries outside Levanthria were not foolish enough to turn away from the powers that can be wielded.*"
Gleya Frederich, Levanthria, A History, 251KR

THIS IS FOR ORJAN.

The words ring through my mind as I plummet over the side of the Zakron's Keep. My decisions to this point are blank; these are memories which I have not yet made, only seeing what the gods allow me to see.

As I am just about to hit the ground, I startle awake, sweat beading on my head. What is it the gods want me to do with this vision? What am I meant to do with Orjan?

I pour myself a drink before walking over to the balcony. The breeze comforts me as it brushes over my skin, my thoughts running through my recurring dream. I have seen the battle at Zakron's Keep time and time again. There are faces within my vision that I recognise, and faces that I do not yet know. No sooner does my vision expand so that I hear Orjan's name, do our paths cross. Where is Laith hiding now? What are he and Jordell planning?

I am far too close to my goals to be deterred now.

Soon, I will provide crucial aid to King Athos Almerion in his victory over Levanthria's Zarubian enemy. It will be enough for him to take me as his queen – if I can survive the battle at Zakron's Keep. But first, I need access to Eltera's forges. I cannot proceed until the Wyverns are disposed of.

I head back to my bed and climb back under the silk, allowing myself into a meditative state before I drift back to sleep.

I am surrounded by flames. A scream cries out around me, and after a moment, I realise it is my own.

"Help me." My voice is that of a young girl's. The nightmare I find myself in is not a vision this time, but a long-suppressed memory.

Flames lick up the walls mercilessly, destroying everything within our home. The raging heat lashes against my face and my heart beats wildly as my fear consumes me.

"Papa!" I call out, but no one calls back. The sound of our home burning is so loud that I need to cover my ears to block it out.

"Papa!"

The table I am under tips over and a soldier whose armour is draped in a yellow tunic with black edges scoops me up.

"I've got you," he tells me.

I bury my head into his chest and wrap my arms around him. "Where's Papa?"

He doesn't answer as he evacuates me from my burning

home. Outside, I lift my head to see soldiers running around helping the other villagers. Flames have engulfed the homes of many others, and I hear cries for help as people are pulled from burning houses.

Horses rush past us in formation and a messenger skids to a halt in front of my rescuer. "Sire! Our scouts have found an army of Barbaraqs nearby!"

The man holding me hands me over to another soldier, frowning. "Barbaraqs? This far north? Get the villagers to safety. They might come back to finish what they started here." He grabs the reins of a horse and pulls himself up.

The small group of soldiers sets off at once. I close my eyes tightly, wishing for the moment to end.

When I open my eyes, it is morning. My bed is sodden with sweat and my bedding lies strewn all over the floor.

There is a knock at the door and a maid enters bearing fresh fruit, water, and a letter. I open the letter at once, eager for news from my spies.

Morgana,

Orjan works quickly and has been tasked with helping Breyton's enforcers. He has even fought in the pits. I heard he is already gaining favour with the Wyverns.

I will keep you posted.

Sparrow

I can't help but smile. It would appear that my plan to infiltrate the Wyverns is already bearing fruit. I have two people on the inside and the Wyverns are none the wiser. It is only a matter of time before my plan comes together and we have access to the forge once more. If my research is correct, with that forge I will be able to harness the properties within ironite like never before. In the meantime, only time will tell what the gods have planned for Orjan and myself. For now, I must wait and see what he does next.

19

ORJAN

For the next few weeks, I trail Grush, serving as an enforcer alongside him. Each person I injure weighs heavy on my mind, but it is what I must do to ensure Rior's safety. To my relief, Trovell does not asked me to fight in the pits again. As agreed, I have sent word to Morgana on two occasions to report on Wyvern actions. All in the hopes of finding Breyton who remains elusive as ever, if he even exists at all.

Today, I find myself with some free time, so I make my way to the shelter. I have not spoken with Rior since the Wyverns recruited me, and I find myself itching for proof that they have kept their word and left him alone.

When I enter the shelter, the room falls silent as stares rain down on me. But when I try to make eye contact with the people, they look away from me. It seems that my reputation as an enforcer has begun to precede me.

Rior emerges from the back room, a small crate of freshly made bread in his arms. When he sees me, I feel a pang of sadness from the disappointment in his eyes. He slides the bread onto the counter and turns to leave without uttering a word to me.

"Rior," I call out, but the boy ignores me. I follow him into the back room. "Rior!"

This time he stops. "What do you want?" There is venom in his voice.

"I wanted to check you are okay."

He scowls as he fetches a cloth and begins to tidy the kitchen. "I am fine."

"You do not seem fine."

"I've heard stories from people coming here, stories about the things you have been doing. Is it true?"

A sense of shame overcomes me. "I do those things to protect you from harm."

"At what cost, Orjan?" His face reddens as he bangs around the kitchen.

"I couldn't let them harm you, Rior."

Rior does not respond as he continues to bustle about. I watch, searching for the right words, but they evade me.

Finally, Rior whirls around to face me. "You are not bound to me, you have no tie. I release you of your burden, Orjan. If hurting other people is what you must do to protect me, then – then I don't want your protection. I'll protect us!" For a boy of such a young age, Rior shows a deep sense of wisdom. "I am ashamed, Orjan. Ashamed that I met you, ashamed of what you are doing, ashamed of you!" He stomps out of the kitchen and heads for the stairs.

"Rior, please. If you want me to stop, then please leave Eltera. It is the only way I know you will remain safe."

"If I leave, who will help our people? Who will provide shelter, food, and warmth to those in need?" Tears fill his eyes. "Just leave, Orjan." His footsteps creek on the old steps as he makes his way upstairs.

I am left alone in the kitchen with nothing but my thoughts. At least the boy is safe. Even if he wants nothing to do with me, at least I can rest knowing that he will come to no harm.

As I make to leave, a familiar figure fills the doorframe. Grush fixes me with a menacing stare, his breathing forced.

"And what do you think you are doing here, Dragon?"

I close my eyes and clench my teeth. It takes every ounce of me not to respond in an antagonising way. "I merely came to check in on the boy, make sure that the Wyverns are staying as true to their word as I am."

Grush steps inside, allowing a handful of his men to pass him and fill the room around us, stopping anyone already here from leaving. "Do you hear that? The dragon questions our word. Tell me, Dragon, has any harm come to Rior?" There is a dangerous glint in his eye.

I remain silent. Over the weeks I've come to recognise when Grush is on the verge, and now is not a good time to provoke his temper.

"I said, has any harm come to Rior?"

He nods at one of his men and they take hold of a woman sitting with a small bowl of soup in her hands. Her clothes are tattered, her face as gaunt as it is pale. I move towards her, but Grush blocks my path.

"Do not make me repeat my question a third time, Dragon."

"No," I answer, not taking my eyes off the woman. "No harm has come to the boy." She stares at me in silent pleading.

Grush nods again and one of the men strike her across her face. She whimpers as she falls back into the chair.

"That's your fault, that." Grush speaks through gritted teeth. "For two reasons. Number one," he elevates his voice loudly, "you came here without permission and insulted our honour. Number two, you did not answer me when I asked you a question. Instead, you look like you're ready to fight me. You still need to be broken in, don't you, Dragon?" His gritted teeth morph into a sinister smile. "This is because of you, Dragon. If you sleep tonight, know in your nightmares that the ordeal this woman will face is down to your actions here tonight."

What little colour is left in the woman's face drains as her skin turns almost translucent, fear etched into her bloodied face. Grush's men drag her up from the ground and she wails and screams as she tries to fight them off. Grush's men simply sneer as they begin tearing at her clothes.

"Stop!" I yell, but Grush rushes into my space and hits me in the stomach. It is enough to take my breath and I stagger back.

"Any more from you and she will not survive the night. Then I'll make a personal visit to Rior."

The others in the room sit by, unsurprised by what they see and reluctant to intervene in the Wyverns' actions.

"Come on, love, we have a long night to get through." He smiles at me once more and all I can imagine is obliterating his head against the counter besides us. "And even more men." He nods at the door and Grush's men drag the half-naked woman from the shelter to gods know where.

My body is so tense that my muscles ache, my bones cracking from the tension. In my heart I just want to follow them outside and destroy them all, but that will not get me near to Breyton nor will it keep Rior or the rest of the shelter safe. I gain control of myself, seething with anger.

Grush smirks, his broken teeth on full display. "There's a good little dragon."

Nearly trembling with rage, I realise that I only have one option.

20

ORJAN

"As we slowly learn about magic once more, the varying kinds of powers are being discovered. Long forgotten energies not drawn upon in these lands for nearly half a millennia. Fire, Ice, Storm, Barrier and Healing are but a few types of spells that can be wielded. What we are learning is that a spell caster can only harness the power of one type of magic, the reason of which we do not know why."

Jordell Torvin, Former priest at the Great Temple, 254KR

I HAMMER on the door of Trovell's office, my blood still boiling from Grush's actions at the shelter. "Trovell, it's Orjan!"

"Enter." Trovell's voice sounds laboured, almost bored, and I swear I hear the man sigh.

I enter with such force that the door almost swings from its hinges as it bounces back from the stone walls, banging loudly in the process.

Trovell frowns at my entrance. "What is the meaning of this insolence?"

Realising I need to tone my behaviour down before I escalate another situation, I hold up my hands as a sign that I mean him no harm. "Apologies, Trovell. I forget my own strength sometimes."

"What is it?" He raises his pointed face from the book he is scribing notes in and inspects me. "It does not take a wise man to realise that something has irked you."

"Grush," I growl. "The man inflicts torment on people for pleasure. Just this moment he and his men are doing unspeakable things to people who have not wronged the Wyverns." My breathing steadies as I get a grip of my temper, a feat far easier knowing that Grush is not in my vicinity.

"I see." Trovell looks up at me from behind the spectacles that sit at the bottom of his nose. "Grush has done a fine job at keeping the people of Eltera in check. He helps make sure that no one steps beyond their means. Without Grush, I am afraid there would be no order."

"Then at least make sure that those who are harmed are only those that have committed crimes. They take what they want from the people, when they want it. A system that will at some point lead to a revolt of some kind."

Trovell studies me for a moment before closing his book, his long, wrinkled fingers resting on top of the leather-bound cover.

"A revolt, you say?" Trovell stands and makes his way to a cabinet in the corner where he removes a bottle of whiskey. "Grush assures me that he has dealt with a member of a group threatening to rise up against us. He said you had quite the hand to play in the maiming of the man."

Shame overcomes me for the part I played in breaking the man's leg that first night with Grush. Since then, I have reluctantly aided him in delivering beatings to the people of this kingdom. I have stopped asking what their crimes were because I would rather not know. I am a shadow of the former knight of Rashouya. What I wouldn't give to be able to return to my kingdom, to be accepted by my kin once again. Instead, I find myself here, cursed by this scaled form with no honour, no dignity, no self-respect. I have fallen such a long way since my days of protecting the royal family. The gods play cruel games indeed. The harder I try, the more those around me pay the consequences. Everywhere I go, I leave nothing but a trail of sorrow and scorn. Is there even any point in trying to do the right thing anymore?

"So, you don't like the way we do things, even though we have kept order since the witch trials went so wrong," Trovell asks whilst pouring whiskey into two glasses.

"I said you run the risk of people rising up. They do as you ask because they are fearful of you. You would command more respect from them if you only punished those that committed true crimes."

"Interesting." Trovell stares out the window into the darkness for a moment before stepping towards me with an outstretched arm, offering me one of the whiskeys. "I will discuss this with Breyton. Grush and the other Wyverns will not be pleased if Breyton agrees. I am not touching the pits though. The Wyverns need it for their entertainment, and it is a good way for people to earn their coin."

"This is all I ask of you. In return, I will continue with our agreement." I take a sip from the whiskey and savour the soft, sweet blend of flavours. It is of far better quality than the whiskeys I have become accustomed to. I stare into the bottom of the glass as I finish its contents, Trovell's frosted face blurred by the base of the glass.

"That is what I am hoping." Trovell grins and a strange sensation overcomes me. My arm feels heavy and the world around me becomes muffled as if everything around me moves in slow motion. As nice as the whiskey was, I find it hard to believe that it would be potent enough to affect me this way so quickly, unless –

"It's poisoned." I stumble back against the wall, finding it difficult to keep focused as Trovell's smile blends into the rest of his facial features.

"No no, what would be the point in poisoning you?" Trovell's voice sounds distant and fractured, his notes deeper than usual.

I take a step towards him but as I plant my foot, my leg buckles and I slam into the ground. My glass shatters to the floor, spraying across the room in front of me. I attempt to lift my head, but its weight is too much, and my eyes begin to fall shut.

A strong smell of vapours erupts up my nose, snapping me back into consciousness. I growl and the young Wyvern in my vicinity is right to quickly get himself out of my range. As I come to, the sound of raucous conversation catches my attention from above.

I am in the base of the pits again.

Jeers greet me as I stumble to my feet. A fat Wyvern catches my attention as he throws his tankard towards me. I catch it with my right hand before it can hit me, staring down at the cretin whose colour drains from his face. Without thinking, I hurl it back at him, and it crashes square into his face. He falls backwards and his comrades laugh at him. When he stands back up, it takes two of them to hold him back. In truth, I welcome the challenge. Let him step into this arena with me, let me show him what I can really do to him.

Trovell clears his throat, and the room falls silent around me. Two Wyverns to my left continue their discussion at an audible volume and Trovell gives them a stern look. One of them, seeing that he is looking, elbows the other and the two of them end their conversation.

Trovell clears his throat before addressing the room. "Dragon has spoken. He asks that we only punish those who have committed crimes."

The Wyverns jeer in disapproval, spitting at me from above.

Trovell stretches out his arms and the room falls silent once more. "I thought about this and, following discussion with Breyton, we agree."

There are grumbles of discontent amongst the ranks. They do not like what they are hearing, but I cannot help but smile. There must be more to it than this though. Why else would Trovell spike my drink and dump me in the pits? The man wants me to fight, but the question is, who?

"There have been rumours of a group rising up against us, and it grows in size. Breyton has declared that we need to keep the people on side, and he has an idea that he thinks you will enjoy."

There is a cheer from the crowd, ringing with uncertain approval.

"Grush, if you will."

Grush shoves a burly man in front of him as the other Wyverns follow with two more people. Those captured have their arms bound behind their backs, their faces blotched and swollen from the recent beatings.

"Kneel!" Grush commands, his intimidating physique enough to make the three prisoners do as they are told.

Kneeling opposite of me on the far side of the pit, the three of them look at me with terror in their eyes.

"These three cowards have committed crimes. All three need to stand and face judgement," Trovell announces. The room falls silent once more as he speaks. "They will face judgement at the hands of the dragon!"

The room begins to cheer loudly, excited by the entertainment they are about to bear witness to.

"Our dragon here will fight one of these men to the death. The others will go free. Which one do you choose to fight, Dragon?"

I scan the three quivering prisoners, none of whom make eye contact with me.

"I will not do this." I elevate my voice so that it echoes around the room above.

Trovell smiles at me and brings his hands together in front of him. "I thought you might say as much. Grush, if you would."

Grush stands behind the young man in the centre and grabs hold of his hair before pulling his head back. In a quick movement, he removes his dagger and drags it across the throat of the red-haired man, whose eyes widen as his neck spills blood.

Grush holds him in place for a few moments as the young man gargles and splutters. The crowd above us cheers wildly.

"Do as Breyton commands, or the remaining two will share the same fate. Further blood spilled due to your inability to do as you are told," Trovell says.

The gods play a cruel game to put me in this position. Either way, blood will be spilled. Who am I to be the judge and executioner?

"What are their crimes?" I ask reluctantly.

"The man whose throat has been slit was caught stealing food from the market," Trovell starts. "The man to your left –" Trovell points at a man of average build with greying hair

–"beat up a member of our Wyvern family, so much so that the victim is now blind in his left eye."

"Please, Dragon, I only sought to protect my daughter from their wandering hands." Grush slams his fist into the side of his head. "No one asked you for your excuses."

I feel a pang of empathy for this man. If his words are true, I do not see how I can punish a man for standing up against these monsters.

"The man on your right solicited company with a lady of the night. Only, once he had received his pleasurable company, he refused to pay. This woman falls under Wyvern protection and the way we see it, this man has committed rape!" The prisoner in question is a portly man with a thick black beard and matted dark hair. His eyes look deeper, unforgiving as they fix onto my own.

The crowd jeers loudly, some beginning to throw their glasses and tankards towards the two men.

"Tell me, Dragon, who will you face? Who will seek judgement and appease the gods, appease Breyton?" Trovell smiles once more, savouring every sickening moment of this.

My mind is made up. With little choice in the matter and the crowd baying for blood, I will have to go along with this repulsive game.

One way or another, I will end Breyton and his cruel reign.

The crowd cheers as I raise my arm and point at the black-bearded man.

Trovell grins. "Fetch this man some armour and a sword. Let's make this an interesting fight."

21

MORGANA

I cannot shake my nightmare from my thoughts as I sit eating chopped fruit the maids have prepared for my breakfast. It has been years since my dreams reminded me of the night I lost my family, the night my father was slaughtered and my sister taken by the Barbaraqs. To this day I do not know the name of my rescuer, the man who led the soldiers that saved the survivors of the attack. Being orphaned at a young age showed me exactly how cruel this world can be; it helped mould me into the person I am today. One that refuses to grow close to people. If I don't become attached, it will not affect me when they pass to the afterlife.

"Lord Wistler is here," a young guard announces to the room. The snake enters, his purple silk tunic reminding me of everything that is wrong with this man. He parades around in his fineries whilst letting this kingdom fall into ruin, allowing this castle to fall into disrepair.

"Morgana, how are you on this fine morning?"

There is something different about the coward today.

Usually he is a quivering wreck of a person, afraid to challenge his own shadow.

"What has brought you to be in such a fine mood?" I ask, finishing the final piece of jarjoba fruit.

"Nothing in particular." Wistler smirks as if reminiscing on something. He lifts a piece of fruit from the table and takes a bite from a vibrant green apple with an audible crunch. "Have you heard from your pet yet? How is he doing with the little errand you sent him on. What was his name again?"

"Orjan? Last I heard he was already gaining favour with the Wyverns." I only have Sparrow's word on this matter, as Orjan's correspondences have been rather vague and inconsistent.

"Oh?" Wistler says, making a face.

I roll my eyes. "What is it?"

"It's just, that isn't what I heard." He moves awkwardly as he pulls a chair out from under the table. I find it strange how he goes from walking in with confidence to suddenly being the Wistler that I am more accustomed to. "Word has reached me this morning that the Wyverns despise him, even though he does as they bid, like an obedient dog." Wistler pours himself some tea and calmly brings the cup to his lips to take an overly loud sip. The way he eats and drinks is as if he were not taught the etiquette of a nobleman.

"What do you mean? Where did you hear this?" I am surprised by my own reaction. It is as if I feel a semblance of concern for a monster that I barely even know.

"Lady Morgana, I still have my own eyes and ears in the streets of Eltera," Wistler answers, leaning back in his chair. "My messenger tells me that Orjan is nothing more than entertainment for the Wyverns. He hands out punishment in the pits to those who have wronged the Wyverns. They have even given him a new name."

"A new name?" This isn't at all what I tasked Orjan to be doing.

"Dragon." Wistler smiles. "Funny old name, but intimidating nonetheless. If word is true, he is brutal in the pits. No one will want to challenge the Wyverns."

I saw first-hand what he was capable of in the markets. The ferociousness that he displayed, his strength, his fury. It nearly matched my own. Maybe that's what I was drawn to that day. He caught my attention before I knew his name after all.

"Dragons are mythical creatures not seen for thousands of years, Wistler."

"The man has a thick hide like a lizard, yet walks these lands and speaks as if human. I think 'dragon' suitably explains him." Wistler looks quite proud of himself which I find somewhat absurd. Why would he be so invested in what the Wyverns have nicknamed Orjan?

"Lord Wistler." The young guard returns and interrupts our conversation. "Scouts have returned from Osar."

Wistler looks somewhat confused by the interruption, and his cheeks redden. "Can't you see that I am in conversation with Lady Morgana?"

"I apologise, sir. My message is urgent," the guard counters, his own cheeks flushed with discomfort.

"Well, what is it?"

"Uster has been attacked. Our scouts send word that little remains of the fishing port. The scouts have said it is savages responsible for the attack. They have left the heads of those slaughtered impaled on pikes."

I curse out loud. "Barbaraqs." This is what happened to my village, as my nightmare reminded me just last night.

"The gods warned me of this attack, yet they were unclear in their message," I say as I bring myself to my feet. My arms tremble where I stand, and the memories of my village come flooding to the forefront of my mind, the smell of blood mixed with the burning embers of our homes. The sound of steel on steel as the soldiers who rescued us clashed with the remaining Barbaraqs.

"Send word to Codrin in Askela!" I demand. "If the Barbaraqs are on their way here then we are going to need reinforcements. With your fractured kingdom, Eltera stands little chance of an assault given its current vulnerable state." I make for the courtyard with haste, the veins in my body aching as my heart beats furiously. I am far more powerful than the last time I saw the Barbaraqs, and I swore then I would make them pay. This is my chance and I intend to take it.

"Morgana, where is it you go?" Wistler asks.

"Tell me your name," I ask the young guard.

"Dante."

"Well, Dante, gather a handful of guards. We head to Uster." If we move quickly, we might be able to follow their tracks. That or come face-to-face with the bastards on our journey.

"Morgana, you will get yourself killed!" Wistler contests, but I have already made up my mind.

"Fetch me a horse!" I call as daylight greets me. A young stable maid fetches a grey steed which is ready for riding, and I quickly hop onto it. To my left, Dante speaks with four other guards who hurriedly ready themselves and scramble for their horses. As tempting as it is, I can't take more guards with me. To do so would leave the castle even weaker, and if the kingdom were to fall, I'd have no chance of getting access to the forge I so desire.

I heel my horse and it neighs wildly as we set off at pace, the wind tangling my hair, my thoughts fixed on the Barbaraqs. If it is them, if it is the same tribe that slaughtered my family, then they will rue the day that they set foot back on the shores of Levanthria. They will know my magic as I send them all to the afterlife.

22

MORGANA

"Just what does it take to have gods look down with such ferocity that they feel the need to interject with this mortal realm. What unspeakable acts needs to be taken in order to find yourself cursed?"
Yuri Crier, Magic And Monsters Volume II, 179KR

MY HORSE PROVES to be strong, and hours pass as we travel hard past the Biterian Plains, seeking to make solid ground as fast as possible beneath the blazing heat of the sun. I remain focused throughout the ride, imagining the things I will do to these people if I manage to find them. Maybe I will use their bodies on which to conduct further experiments. Or maybe I will simply lay waste to each and every one of them.

Our horses begin to tire as the sun shrinks, bringing with it a welcome reprieve from the harsh heat and dryness of the Biterian Plains. In the distance just beyond the hills, smoke trails into the sky, and my heart beats a little faster.

"Over there!" Dante calls, having spotted the smoke for himself. "Be ready, men. We do not know what awaits us."

The closer we draw to Uster, the more the stench of burning cedar greets us. A fog sits on the horizon, but it is not one brought about by nature. This is made by man.

"Secure the perimeter," Dante commands. "Draw your swords."

When we enter Uster, we are met by an eery quietness uncharacteristic for a trading port. Houses smoulder with embers from the attack, and bodies lie strewn on the ground. Those that have survived scramble to aid others in need. There are many injured, many dead, but there is one thing I find curious.

"Where are the guards?" I ask.

Dante rides besides me and examines the ruins of the village. "I do not know."

A dampness in the air following a downpour of rain has lent its aid to quell the flames, though smoke still rises from the thatched roofs, threatening to reignite at any moment. Some are collapsed in on themselves, others are left with gaping holes. Those with stone walls suffered minimal damage compared to those that were erected with wood. If my family had been able to afford stone walls, would they have survived all those years ago?

"You there, where are the guards?" I beckon to a portly man who carries an injured woman in his arms.

"You tell me. We were defenceless. We didn't stand a chance against such savages. They were nowhere to be seen, they left us."

With a flick of my wrist, I rid the woman of her pain, and her grimaced cries stop.

"You – you have magic," the man states, his eyes widening. It must be the first time he has witnessed it.

"Her pain will ease but her wounds will still need tending to if she is to survive this day," I tell him. "I suggest you move quickly." I could transfer her wounds, even heal them, but it is not worth tapping into the reserves of my magic.

"Thank you," he says, then continues on.

"One more thing," I say, stopping him in his tracks. "Where is the guard post?"

He nods past us down the street. "Their post is down by the harbour. If you see any of them, tell them the gods will curse them on this day for their lack of action."

"I assure you if they have allowed this to happen, they will wish it was the gods that cast down judgement when I have brought my wrath upon them."

I dig my heels into the sides of my horse and we set off down the street at a canter, the broken village dragging up remnants of my past like a fractured window. When I arrive at the guard post, there is a row of unarmed guards lined up on the ground, their faces frozen in fear as they were executed together. I count seven, meaning there are far more unaccounted for.

Bringing my horse to a stop, I dismount and drop to the ground. The guards' blood has washed down the street, leaving a crimson stream that trickles to the wooden jetty and into the ocean.

"Help me," a hoarse voice gasps, startling me.

As I look around for the source, I spot a female guard sitting against the doorway to the guard tower. Her long blond hair is matted with blood, her hands clasped around a gushing wound in her stomach.

It is only out of need of information that I move towards her. When I kneel beside her, I am struck by her eyes. They are like crystal, a sharp blue. Not unlike someone I used to know.

I bite down on the memories of my past, forcing my thoughts to one side. I cannot allow them to distract me. "Tell me what happened," I say.

"The guards," she splutters, blood spraying from her mouth. "They were infiltrated."

I frown. "By the Barbaraqs?" Barbaraqs aren't exactly known for discrete battle tactics.

"Not the Barbaraqs," she croaks. "Wyverns."

I fight to hide my shock as I try to make sense of this.

"They lined everyone up," she continues. "Those of us who would not do as they said." Her sunken eyes drift to the pile of bodies that lie just behind me. Her eyes well with tears and she sobs, coughing up more blood in the process. "They let them in, they let the Barbaraqs dock their ships. And then they let them free on Uster to do as they wish." The woman bows her head back and squeezes her eyes as she grimaces from her pain. "Why? Why would they do this, why would the Wyverns let these savages into Levanthria? There is nothing good that can come of this."

"Why indeed," I mutter under my breath. "Let me see your injuries."

The woman raises her hands from her abdomen. I have a strong stomach, but even I have to suppress a wretch as the extent of her injuries are revealed to me. Her innards sit on full display, strings of fat and muscle all that prevent them from splaying everywhere.

"Please, help me," she begs, her skin a ghostly pallor.

"Do you know where they went?"

"I heard one of the Wyverns say they were heading north to make camp, that they were to wait there until they got the command from Breyton."

Why in the gods' names would Breyton bring these savages back to Levanthria's shores?

Focusing my magic, I place my hand on the woman's to soothe her pain.

"Th – thank you," she says, her eyes softening. She closes her eyes and releases one last breath, free from pain, free from this torturous world.

I stand, taking in what is left of Uster. It will take years to rebuild what has been destroyed by the Barbaraqs, by the Wyverns. Small, narrow boats line the port, the front of them carved into the heads of what look like dragons. The masts are singular in the centre of the boats with lines of oars protruding from the sides. The boats look more basic than our fleet, but judging by the shape, these ships are built for speed, not for endurance. Wasting no time with a rough gauge on where they have made camp, I rush to my horse and gallop back up the hill towards the entrance to Uster. When I return to my group, Dante is tending to the injured and directing the other men.

"Where are you going?" he asks as I rush past him.

"North, where they make camp. We cannot allow this attack to go unpunished," I call back, my focus on the land ahead of me.

As I look over my shoulder, I see Dante rushing to his own steed, the other guards doing the same. I don't care how long we need to ride for. We will find them, and I will do what I must.

23

ORJAN

I am a monster.

I have become the very thing that the Wyverns call me: a dragon. Accepting sacrifices as if it appeases the gods when in truth it only appeases the men and woman who sit cheering around the pit.

I stare into the bottom of my tankard, hoping that with each mouthful, my darkened thoughts will wash away. Instead, they worsen just like the hatred that I hold for myself. Hopefully the harm I've caused to a few will protect many. That is, if Breyton is a man of his word and sticks to the agreement. But in truth, I have seen nothing to show me that Breyton is a man of honour. All I see is a group of men and women who took advantage of a bad situation with the promise of improving things. How power corrupts people even with the best of intentions.

I take another gulp of my ale and see the many eyes of the room searching over me. People speak in hushed voices, some out of fear, some having heard the stories. Some are simply transfixed at the sight of my scaled skin, my yellow eyes, and my jagged teeth. A couple of men sit playing cards at the far side of the room, laughing with one another. One of the men slams a card down in frustration whilst the older player laughs at his misfortune, a pipe protruding from his lips. The sight draws me to a vague memory of Voraz, to the night when I first met Ulrik. It was from there where we set sail to Treventine, it is there where I foolishly put myself forward and received this curse.

"Fucking Vireo!" I muse loudly as I bring my drink back up to my mouth. After all, it was that day in Askela that led to me being in Voraz in the first place. That piece of shit is the cause of all my woes, the reason I lost Laith. What I wouldn't give for an opportunity to be in the pits with *him*. He would feel my wrath, my retribution. That is a man who deserves a fool's court in order to distribute punishment, and one I would gladly play a hand in.

I stand from my table and take the last few gulps of my ale before stumbling towards the bar. My plan to submerge myself in drink to forget the day is slowly working. I knock into a couple of people in my way but no one dares challenge me. I am not proud of the fear on their faces, but I use this to my advantage to be left alone.

"Another," I growl as I slam my tankard on the bar. An older man with a grey beard attends to me.

"Don't you think you have had enough, Drag –"

"Call me fucking Dragon and I will remove your tongue."

"I didn't mean to offend you," the barman stutters as he hastily pours me another pint of ale.

A woman stands opposite the bar, her eyes fixed on me. When my eyes land on her, she quickly averts her gaze, but I am already drawn to the strange amber colouring of her eyes. Her cheek is bruised, and it looks as though she is smarting a black eye. Her hair is short as if cut by her own hand, dark brown in colour. She stands out from the other customers with her lightweight leather armour and a sturdy looking cauldron on her right shoulder.

"Don't you know it is rude to stare," I growl.

"Apologies, I meant no offence."

"Well, that is precisely what you have caused." I bang my hand on the bar and startle some of the locals into complete silence. "I have just about had enough of everyone in this blasted kingdom!" I reach for my freshly filled tankard and take a huge glug.

The people in the tavern do not know where to look, and the barman edges to the back door.

The woman places an arm in front of the barman, blocking him, then turns to me. "You don't need to get the Wyverns," she tells the innkeeper. "Why don't you take my coin and buy this man a drink from me." Her eyes catch my own as she takes a coin from her pocket and places it on the bar in front of her. "There is no quarrel and there will be no need for assistance."

The woman is confident but still on edge. I don't blame her. These days, I hardly know which way my temper will sway myself.

"You want to be careful staring at monsters, you may find yourself turning to stone," I grumble as I take another sip of my drink.

When the woman moves closer to me, I notice she is carrying an injury to her right leg as she limps heavily to the vacant chair beside me.

"I did not mean to cause alarm." Her voice is strained, as if the pain in her leg is much worse than she lets on. "I know you seek solitude in your drinking but trust me when I say that it will lead you down a dark path."

I can't help but smirk. "Miss, I have walked down blackened streets long before this night. I have drowned myself many times over in order to escape my thoughts. You know nothing of the darkness that I walked through to get here. That sky outside, the darkest depths of the ocean – it pales in comparison to the darkness that is within my heart."

"I have been where you stand," she says.

"Oh? Do you have scales, too?"

"I have carried my own darkness within me." Her amber eyes become distant as she perches herself on a barstool next to me. "Drowning yourself in ale may grant you a brief reprieve, but it will not help you face the demons you hide from."

The woman's words cut deep. I reach for my tankard once more, but she places her hand delicately on top of my forearm. Her touch jolts me, reminding me of Zerina when I first joined her and Ulrik's crew as we sought the Fountain of Youth.

"You don't need to do this, Orjan, you need to fight those demons."

"Not tonight I don't." I move my arm away and scoop up my tankard before downing the remainder of the drink in one gulp.

"Very well, Orjan. But enough of this swill. Petor, give us a bottle of rum, two glasses."

She leads me over to a table by the fire and I take a seat opposite her. The fire kisses my cheek, yet it brings me little warmth. She has my attention, and for once it might be nice to have some company.

"Tell me, what is your name?" I ask.

"Sparrow."

24

MORGANA

"High Priestess Caitel Jentaro is considered to have been one of the first spell casters of this age to ignore the Kings order that banned the use of magic across Levanthria. Caitel Jentaro refused to obey this order, despite the violence being shown to all spell casters and instead put her life in jeopardy in order to use her healing magic to aid others. This was not without fear however and Caitel had to remain hidden, setting safe, sterile areas for those who were sick or injured to heal. When the last Great War raged, Caitel joined the battle but refused to take lives only save them. It was after her death that The Great Temple elevated her status to High Priestess to recognise how she had continued to put the needs of others before herself."

Boraf Voretti, Scribe to the Great Temple, 203KR

THE NIGHT IS dark and unassuming. There is no moon on this night, lending us plenty of darkness to remain hidden until the opportune moment presents itself. Ahead of us there is a dim light towards a cluster of tall trees, a perfect place for a camp.

"Is that where they make camp?" Dante asks, his horse panting heavily from the journey.

My own steed managed to make it here with little fuss following the burst of energy I gave it, but the others straggled behind me.

"We should leave the horses here, Morgana. It will allow us the element of surprise."

"I agree. We will continue on foot. When we reach the camp, you attack on my command."

Dante nods and we hitch our horses to the nearby trees before beginning our walk to the Barbaraq camp. It doesn't take long before the sound of the wind is replaced with the sound of the Barbaraqs cheering and singing. They make no attempt to hide their camp at all, which makes them either brave or foolish. As we draw closer, my heart begins to thunder in tandem with the beating of the drums they are dancing to. Slowly their camp becomes more than a distant memory. They are here. The people responsible for altering my life forever are here.

It is a large encampment, with only a few sentries acting as lookouts on the outer edge. We are still not close enough to see what happens in the centre of camp, where the noise comes from.

"What now?" Dante asks. "They far outnumber us. It would be madness to attack their camp with so few."

I have only one thing on my mind, and I do not care for the guards who have accompanied me on this journey. Their lives mean nothing to me. I stare at one of the sentries and I begin to search my mind for my magic. The spell I plan on casting is one that I have not yet fully harnessed, but I hope I can use this to my advantage.

My mind feels fluid, as if my vision travels on the breaths of the wind, like a feather. I maintain my focus as I mutter words under my breath, the soothing sensation of magic coursing through my body. My vision reaches the sentry and within a moment it is as though I am looking out over the field with his eyes. I breathe in the smell of smoke and meat that must be cooking nearby. The stench sends pangs to my stomach. This warrior must not have eaten for some time, possibly not since the attack on Uster. I exhale deeply and gather the bearings of my new body, waiting for a moment for the initial dizziness to pass. I have only cast this spell on a few occasions, mainly on small animals and once with a prisoner. On both occasions I was only able to keep my connection for a short period of time, so I know I need to move fast.

Behind me I hear the drums and song of the Barbaraqs as they celebrate their incursion. Looking down, I inspect the hands I am now in possession of. They are worn and heavily calloused. These are aged hands, experienced hands. I glance to my right where another sentry stands guard, his war axe strapped to his back. He looks like he's half asleep, no doubt exhausted from the day's fight.

I cast a quick glance around me and see that no one is in our vicinity, so I seize my opportunity and move towards the Barbaraq.

"Yuuri, what are you doing?" he asks, but before he can act, I grip him by the throat and swing behind him, bending my arm around his neck. The body I possess has much strength and the man tries to struggle against me but the element of surprise weighs heavily in my favour. He grabs hold of my arm as he tries to pull himself free, but I am too strong for him. I squeeze tightly until his arms begin to fall limp and I hear the crunch of his neck breaking under my brute force.

My teeth clenched and breathing laboured, I allow the Barbaraq to slump to the floor and I spit on his body out of disgust. My anger is rising, and I know I must make haste if I am to make good of this body. I head into the camp where I see a group of people in a large circle around a central fire. They dance and sing, taking part in whatever ceremonial savagery they wish. They drink wine and spirits pillaged from Uster, men and women grabbing one another as they make their way back to their makeshift shelters. Their clothing is as though they have been brought up in the wild. They wear slipshod leathers formed from animal pelts. Most are bare chested, with only a few wearing animal hides to keep warm. Some walk around with little covering their modesty and heavily tattooed skin.

My head grows drowsy, and I can feel the owner of this body begin to fight me for control as I continue to survey my surroundings. The only other sentries I see are on the far side of the camp. The rest have dropped their guard as they dance, drink, and engage in all manner of debauchery.

A large man pushes his way through the crowd, and something about him is familiar. He stands a good foot taller than most within this tribe, their ranking most likely brought about purely by who is the strongest. His bald head is tattooed with a thick black stripe that runs from his forehead over the top of his head and right down the centre of his back.

My vision shakes as I begin to lose control of this host. With little time to spare I spin away from the group and head back to the spot where the sentries have taken up post. Checking my surroundings again, I remove a dagger from my belt.

I stare at the blade for a second as my vision blurs. Taking in a deep breath, I plunge the blade into my abdomen. Searing pain engulfs me. I feel my skin tear as I slide the blade to the right for good measure before twisting the blade, leaving this host body no chance of survival.

Then it is as if my consciousness is sucked away and drawn back to my own body in a matter of seconds. It is most disorienting, and I find myself feeling faint as a rush of heat makes its way up my face.

"What was that?" Dante asks, his voice elevated. He is clearly not used to seeing such magic in close proximity.

"That is only a little of what I am capable of." I hope this display of my power will encourage them to fight even though we are outnumbered. My eyes roll back suddenly, and my body convulses as if I myself have been possessed this time. This is not the first time this has happened to me however, and I embrace the sensation, I embrace whatever vision the gods bestow on me. However poor their timing is.

Screams ring out. The village around me is in flames. I am brought back yet again to the night of the Barbaraq attack on my village. This time I am stood outside my house alongside my sister and my father. I hold my sister's hands tightly. She is younger than I, her brown hair braided as best my father could. We look around, searching for where our attackers are. Then the war cries reach us, a scream mixed with a roar. It hits me in my core, and I have never known fear like this. A man moves across in front of us, his bare chest covered in ink and warpaint. He holds a hatchet above his head as he strikes down a woman nearby. My father doesn't hesitate. Already clutching his sword, he steps toward the Barbaraq warrior and brings his blade down on him. The warrior blocks this and kicks our father in his stomach, causing him to fall in front of us.

"Get as far away as you can!" he demands as he gets back to his feet. Our father is a farmer, not a warrior, but he fights with honour as he engages our enemy once more.

"No, father! We can't."

"Go!" he roars as he begins exchanging blows with our attacker. The war cries around us grows louder and louder.

My sister cries, terrified at the spectacle before us. We have never been exposed to such violence. I pull at her arm, but she is rooted to the spot, frozen in fear.

"Come, Ferelda, we need to leave."

She pulls back against me. "But Papa!" Her face is coated in a layer of ash, small streaks forming where her tears run.

The sound of metal on metal rings out as our father battles to protect us. Hearing the cries of Ferelda, he turns. "Go, now!"

The distraction hinders him and the Barbaraq warrior spins before hammering his axe into our father's stomach.

"Papa!" Ferelda screams and lets go of my hand, running into our house.

My heart breaks in that moment. The sound of the chaos around us dulls down to nothing more than muffled screams as our father drops to his knees and blood pools in his mouth. The Barbaraq pulls back his axe one last time and brings it down on Father's head. He drops to the floor, his eyes wide with shock, staring straight at me. My body shakes. I am bereft with grief, my heart thundering against my chest like a wild storm. Then a scream calls from our house and it grabs my attention immediately. Ferelda. My eyes drift upwards and I see the cause of the screams. The roof has caught fire.

"Ferelda!" I have no time to grieve for my father as the smoke starts to seep out from below our front door. As soon as I enter, my lungs fill with smoke.

"Ferelda!" I cough and splutter, gasping for air. Thick smoke fills the room, making it difficult to see anything.

The ceiling above me grumbles loudly and I dive under the table as it comes crashing down on top of me, pinning me to the spot. The heat is unbearable. I call out my sister's name over and over again, to no answer. Then I see something I have not noticed before in this nightmare, in this memory. The Barbaraq is near the front door, standing over my father's dead body. He turns to leave, revealing a large striped tattoo that runs down the back of his head and his back.

I snap back from my vision and it is clear to me in an instant why the gods have brought me here. The man who killed my father, the man responsible for my sister's death, is the leader of this tribe.

My blood burns, and every muscle in my body becomes taut with tension. A rage rises within me and I lose all sense of self-control. I clench my hands around the grass where I kneel and I take in a deep breath.

Then I stand.

"What is it?" Dante asks.

I don't answer. With every ounce of my energy, I set off at pace towards the Barbaraq camp. My anger consumes me. I have no semblance of a plan. All I know is that the man responsible for my miserable life is just ahead of me. One of us will not make it through this night.

25

MORGANA

I enter the camp at a faster pace than my trailing guards, drawing on my magic to increase my durability. I am not thinking, I am solely in the moment, not caring for my safety.

I reach the deceased sentry and scoop up the bloodied dagger that sits by his fallen hand. The hilt is sticky and warm, but I squeeze it tightly as I head towards the centre of the camp, the dirt scratching under my feet. If not for the beating drums, they would be aware of my assault. And I want them to know that I am here. I want them to know the fury of a woman who had everything taken at such a young age, by their hands. I pant heavily, not from fatigue but by pure, unrivalled rage. I sprint into the middle of their camp.

Women from Uster are being paraded like livestock, their clothes torn, their faces and bodies bloodied by whatever acts these savages have been carrying out. The crowd is cheering, and a younger warrior calls out in satisfaction, his face painted and tattooed. He wears the fur of an animal like a coat. He is closest to me, and he is the first to receive my fury. Moving like an assassin, I draw my dagger across his throat. His gargled breaths are drowned out by the beating drums which I feel hammer against my chest as every beat rings out.

By the time I bury my dagger into the shoulder of the next Barbaraq, they notice my presence. The woman I have just killed drops, her mouth agape with shock as I remove my embedded blade. The crunch of her collarbone is most satisfying.

Two Barbaraqs move towards me. One is armed, the other is not. I hurl my dagger at the first warrior, slamming it into his chest. He is dead before he hits the ground. The second Barbaraq falters for a moment but seems to take confidence in me now being unarmed. If only they knew that now I am unarmed, I am even more dangerous.

I stretch out my arm and stop him in his tracks, paralysing him with my magic. I begin to draw on his energy as I take his life force for my own, and his skin cracks and dries, much to the shouts of disapproval from everyone else.

Dante and the four other guards reach me and dive straight into battle with the circling warriors. Steel against steel rattles loudly as they begin trading blows with one another.

One of the guards falls as an axe is brought down on his head, his blood spraying out like a fountain. Seeing a gap in the formation, I rush through and fire at the centre of the party. It is here where the chieftain waits.

A dust cloud forms between us as I stop to weigh up my actions. I need to challenge him directly. If the other warriors get involved, I will not be able to defend myself from so many. The chieftain stands unfazed by my actions so far. He is powerfully built, far bigger than I recall from my vision, his hulking framed decorated with chiselled muscles. He removes his fur-lined jacket and kneels to pick up his war hammer. He rests this on his shoulder for a moment and raises his hand for his people not to enter the fray.

I let out a cry of anger as I charge down the chieftain. Everything I have become, everything I have learned, comes down to this moment. The chieftain is alarmed by my speed and drops his hammer from his shoulders, gripping it with both hands. He takes a wild swing at me, but I push back his weapon as if my arms are metal. I fire magical energy at him which connects with his chest, and he stumbles back a couple of steps before regaining his composure. A spell like that would take down most, but somehow he is still standing. He takes a swing of his hammer and tries to bring it down on my head from above, but I refuse to meet the same fate as my father. I jump back only just in time before he takes another wild lunge. I fire another blast of energy at him, and he uses his hammer to block this. Then I fire another and another. With each blast, my anger rises, growing more and more vicious with my attacks.

The chieftain begins to stumble back as he grows tired from waving his hammer around. I run towards him and leap through the air. Channelling another wave of energy, I let it engulf my arms like hot fire over metal before unleashing it. It connects with his left shoulder, removing flesh and muscle. He drops his weapon, his mangled shoulder no longer able to bear the weight of his war hammer. I fire another blast into his other shoulder. His blood rushes from his wounds but he stands unyielding and stony-faced before me, grimacing with pain.

"You took everything from me!" I scream as I run towards him, firing another blast of my magic into his legs. His legs buckle beneath him and his knees hit the dirt. He lets out a scream of pain as I clasp my hands around either side of his chiselled face. It feels as though I grasp rough stone between my palms. I draw on his life force, having used a vast amount of magic. There are gasps of horror from the rest of the camp as the chieftain begins to convulse violently in my hands, his face becoming ashen. The warmth of his life drifts up my arms, pulsating as the deep ache from magic use fades. As the throbbing pain lessens, I increase the amount of pressure I am applying. The chieftain lets out a rasping, gargling noise as blood seeps from his eyes and runs down his nose, turning his beard crimson. Roaring from the pain, he struggles but his strength wavers until he draws his final breath. His skin grows weathered, his muscular frame no more. The hands he has clasped around mine fall limply away, and I push his head to the side. Panting heavily, I turn to face the rest of the camp.

They look on in horror and I assume they have never come across magic before, let alone the kind of force that I possess. I stare into the many eyes that now greet me and prepare myself to use my magic again on them. I will strike every one of them down if I need to. It is no less than what they deserve.

A shrill scream rings out as a young woman runs from the crowd, her dark, auburn hair braided back over the top of her head. Her lightly freckled cheeks are awash with tears, and she wears hide-strapped pants, with only a small top that just about covers her modesty. Her chiselled physique is one that I am becoming accustomed to with the Barbaraqs. She rushes towards me, and I ready myself to strike her, but she drops her hatchet as she diverts towards the chieftain. She slides onto her knees, raising a cloud of dust around her as she raises his head towards her.

Is she his bride? He looks to have a number of years on her, but these savages may take young brides. Perhaps she is his daughter. She lets out a scream as she seeks to comfort him in a tongue that I do not recognise. She lifts his arm before letting go and it falls limp as if she is checking for signs of life. Her tears cascade, falling from her nose onto the chieftain's dishevelled head. She lowers her forehead down to his and closes her eyes before letting out another scream of anguish. Then she lifts her head and her eyes fix onto me, the grief in her eyes turning to hate-filled anger that would rival my own.

I can't help but let out a wry smirk at the pain she feels. The man's fate is no less than he deserves for what he has done to me and many others. I have avenged my fallen father and sister. To the afterlife with the rest of this honour-less tribe.

The woman lowers the chieftain's head slowly to the ground and brushes her hand over his face to close his eyes. She brings herself back to her feet all the while keeping her eyes fixated on me. I stare back, readying myself for another fight.

"I slaughtered your chieftain like you slaughter our villages. Unless you want to share the same fate, I suggest you leave." My voice is as stern as ever. I have the gods on my side, after all.

A sudden pull on my arm draws my attention away from her.

"We must make haste!" It is Dante, his face decorated with the blood of the fallen. Behind him, the rest of our guards lie dead on the ground. "There are too many."

Has he not seen what I am capable of? But I came here to kill the chieftain, and I have achieved that. If I were to now lose my life, it would be pointless. This is not the fate bestowed upon me by the gods.

Dante pulls me again, and this time I follow. To my

surprise, none of the Barbaraqs attack us as we make our way through. The only words I hear are the ones of the young woman who shouts out at us as we make our leave.

"Forten grudu druda!" she screams. "I will find you!" she repeats, and I am surprised that she can in fact speak our tongue.

None of the Barbaraqs follow.

26

ORJAN

"Jonah continues to fight against my methods of persuasion, I offer him treasures that he could have only dreamed of as a child, yet he still resists. I can't help but feel that he knows more than he is letting on, that he knows exactly what I want to do with the magical properties within ironite ore. If I can unlock those properties then I will become a truly unstoppable force."

Diary entry of Morgana, 254KR

THE INNKEEPER'S reluctance to put any more logs on the fire tells me that it is nearing time for us to call it a night.

"What are you thinking about?" Sparrow slurs, nearly knocking her tankard over as she places it onto the table.

"I drink to forget, I do not drink to draw on painful memories," I answer, dragging my eyes from the fire. "It has been some time since I spent an evening in the company of another."

"What happened to you?" Sparrow asks. I know she means the curse.

I stare into the flames, and they remind me of the naval ship that Zerina sank on our journey to Treventine. For two years I have wandered Levanthria alone, cursing the gods for what they have done to me. For the situation I am in now, for the harm I have caused.

"Many moons ago, when the Rashouyan pact was in place, I was a knight of the crown. I held honour and prestige, at a young age too. By my mid twenties I had amassed land and fortune for my duties to the then Queen Sallussen. I was renowned for my bravery, for being duty-bound, for the lives I had saved." My voice rasps as the crackling of the fire further dampens. Sparrow's eyes remain fixed onto me, and I wonder for a moment if I should delve into my past. After all, it is this that I have avoided for such a long time.

"It sounds like it was a good life."

"It was. I was a good man. I enjoyed the fruits of my labours, the bounties that I collected for ridding evil people from our land, the occasional demon. Nothing I had faced prepared me for the events that occurred in a small village to the northeast of the Biterian Plains, only a three-day ride from here. I led an envoy to Levanthria, bearing a proposition from our Queen Sallussen for your then new King Athos Almerion. The seas had been kind to us, the journey not arduous at all. All the signs were there that the gods were on our side. We hoped to convey our message to King Athos and unite The Levanthrian and Rashouyan kingdoms. Our combined forces would have been the envy across the word, it would have ensured that no foreign armies would dare step onto our lands. We would have all been safe."

The memories of what could have been come burning to the forefront of my mind. "The Barbaraqs, the savages had raided a village that our envoy was passing. Seeing the smoke and flames, I ordered our envoy to divert. After all, there would be innocents there. We were too late when we arrived. The village was in ruins and many had been slaughtered."

I wince at the memory before taking another drink of my ale. "I had been in battle countless times, but nothing could prepare me for the brutality that we bore witness to on that evening. We rescued who we could. I myself recall pulling a youngster from their burning home. She had lost everything, and my heart broke for her. An anger rose in me, and I knew in an instant that this tribe of lawless, honour-less brutes needed to pay for what they had done. Our scouts found them heading south, to return to the shores. Whatever they had come for, they had gotten, and they were leaving. I commanded my envoy to follow me, leaving a handful of men and women to help the rest of the survivors. My anger guiding me, I led our envoy after the Barbaraqs and that was the start of everything. We underestimated them. *I* underestimated them. They slaughtered every one of my soldiers. I sent them all to an unnecessary death because of my anger."

"And the queen's proposal for the king?" Sparrow asks.

"It never reached him. I went back to the village, distraught by our losses. My soldiers turned on me, they blamed me. The envoy returned to Rashouya to report back to Queen Sallussen and return with more soldiers. I was banished on the spot, my honour rightfully lost in an instant. By the time the envoy returned, time had passed and King Athos Almerion had taken a wife. I bore the blame for the failings. I had disgraced my kingdom."

A steady lump forms in my throat and my eyes begin to sting, but I fight back the tears. I deserve to be in this state. "I turned to drink and gambling, existing purely to wallow in my misery. Each day I woke to find I owed money to men that you do not wish to owe money to."

I laugh to myself as I stare into my near emptied tankard. The embers of the fire are almost extinguished as I have tried to extinguish these memories. But they remain etched, firmly into my mind, despite how much I try, how much I drink. I cannot forget.

"It is fated. Twice I have attempted to get my life back on track and that is what ultimately led me to this curse. I gave up the drink, even took on a squire. An old gambling debt came back to haunt me and once again I found myself humiliated for all to see. I ended up on Voraz, drinking and gambling until a young pirate and a witch took a game on me and let me sail with them."

Beside us, the flames in the hearth finally die.

"I stopped drinking. I slowly found myself bonding with the crew and forming relationships. I took on this curse willingly so that the crew could access a long-forgotten treasure, but taking the curse had consequences that far surpassed my expectation. When the madness of the curse consumed me, I took the life of the captain, my friend. And although the crew did not blame me for this, his young sister did. Her grief warped her mind and I fear the darkened path she now walks. I was cast out on the shores just south of Levanthria. You see, even when I try to help people, to try and make a difference, I only make things worse for everyone. Even now I do unspeakable things in the name of honour, all to protect a young boy I barely know. A young boy who can't look me in the eyes because of the monster I have become, not just on the outside. Even now, I fear that his safety and that of his keeper is not guaranteed."

"It sounds to me like you still hold honour, Orjan. Many other men would have stopped trying by now."

Nothing she says can even begin to help me find redemption. "Everything I touch turns to ash, no different from the logs in this fire," I tell her. I have tried to walk a better path, but look at the trauma that follows me. Laith, Ulrik, Rior . . . They would be better off having not crossed paths with me.

"Don't give up faith. The true testament of a man is his willingness to continue to help others despite the consequences. It sounds selfless to me." Sparrow finishes her pint and slams her tankard onto the table.

"But the more I try, the worse I make things. The gods truly hate me, they must."

"Or maybe this a test that they give you now, to see the path you walk. This could be your redemption." Her smile is alluring but the rest of her features are hazy through intoxication. "I am not innocent in the manner of which I come to be here."

I cast her a sceptical look.

"I find myself in my own situation. Both options I face seem to offer me death at the end of the path."

"What do you mean?" I ask.

She hesitates. Then, through hastened breaths, she continues. "I was sent by the Wyverns to kill Morgana. I was a guard, had been for a few years. My husband had a debt to Breyton. They said if I did as they asked that they would remove the debt."

"And if you didn't?"

"They would kill my husband and my son. I nearly managed it, you know, but that Morgana is a powerful sorceress. She subdued me and had me taken to the dungeons."

I am all too familiar with these dungeons. The dank,

repugnant smell is unforgettable, clinging to my memories just as easily as it stuck to my tunic.

There are few people left in the room now, and our hushed words feel far louder in the empty bar. The innkeeper wipes down tables whilst we continue our discussion.

"She tortured me," Sparrow says. Her eyes become distant and the purplish, swollen bags under her eyes seem to become more apparent to me as she thinks back to her time in the dungeon. "The things she did, the pain she inflicted. My leg still has not healed. She would cut me, then heal me and do it all again. I was desperate. I had no option but to agree to what she demanded of me. I just wanted her to stop. I couldn't go on anymore."

Before me sits a broken woman, one who has crumbled through a drunken conversation.

"What did she ask of you?"

"She told me to keep an eye on you. I have kept her informed, but I fear it is only a matter of time before Morgana has me killed, or Breyton does. If the Wyverns realise I am reporting back to her, they will slaughter my family, and they will make me watch." She pauses and stares through me as if I am a ghost, as if she is able to see what sits behind me. "I tried to assassinate her, she tortured me, and I agreed to feed back information on you. The sorceress does not know mercy. I dread to think what she will do with me when I serve no purpose."

"It would seem we are both between a rock and a hard place. Twisted by our situations." I ponder this for a moment, my eyes becoming heavy as a combination of intoxication and tiredness kicks in. The torment on Sparrow's face is apparent.

"Sparrow, I know all too well the dark actions we can be

forced to make in order to keep others safe. I think your situation is even harder given that your heart belongs to the people being threatened." I exhale deeply and gather myself for a moment before standing to leave.

"Wait!" Sparrow demands.

The only people left in the room are Sparrow, myself, and the innkeeper who stands by the door. He looks at me before pushing the latch into place.

"We needed to wait until the last people left. We don't want our conversation feeding back to the Wyverns."

My stomach plunges. Have I been set up?

I growl at the innkeeper in a menacing manner. I would not like to see him try and stop me from leaving.

"Trust me when I say that I do not wish to fight you," he tells me as if reading my thoughts. "The locking of this door is to stop people coming in, not to prevent you from leaving. I heard what you did to Heath. The man nearly lost his leg. I would be a fool to cross you."

Shame washes over me once more over my actions and how many people I have hurt, and not just since I landed at the gates of Eltera.

"We are trying to build something, Orjan," Sparrow says. "We want to overthrow the Wyverns. If we focus on this, we can worry about Morgana afterwards."

"And how exactly do you intend to do this?"

"This is not the first time our paths have crossed, Orjan. The night that you burst into Heath's house and broke his leg."

It dawns on me. I didn't directly see her, but Grush referenced her. "You are Heath's wife."

She smiles at me. "I am. And we want you to join our rebellion."

27

MORGANA

"Wistler, Wistler!" My voice echoes in the hall as I arrive back to the relative safety of the castle. The pictures of former kings and queens line the walls of the hall, their eyes searching over me as if they understand the darkened path that I walk.

"Wistler!" I call once more, frustrated at the need to repeat myself. A stream of light filters through the windows into the main hall, as if the gods themselves kiss the gilded throne that is decorated with jewels and covered in soft purple velvet. As the light casts over it, I find myself wondering what it would be like to rule these kingdoms. To have the whole of Levanthria bend to my will.

I saunter towards it and place my hand on one of the arms. The metal is cold to the touch, and I grasp it in my palm before turning to sit down. Exhausted, I lean back and let the warmth of the sun kiss my face, savouring the silence that greets me in this moment. For the first time in a while, I feel a sense of calmness and peace, and I wish I could remain in this moment.

"What is it you wish to tell me?" Wistler pulls me back

into the room with his shrill voice. "By the gods, Morgana you look as though you have spent the night in the local taverns. The pits, even." Wistler's eyes widen at my appearance.

I glance down at my once emerald-green dress, which is now torn and shredded, coated in mud and dust from my ride to the Barbaraq camp.

"Where on earth have you been?" Wistler snaps his fingers and a young maid rushes to his side at once, her long blond hair pushed back with a black band. Her timid temperament is emphasised by her trembling arms as she approaches him.

"Sire," she says, offering him a curtsy.

"Fetch Lady Morgana some water and fresh fruit. And send for a healer at once."

Wistler's assertiveness takes me by surprise. He is not his usual bumbling self. "I do not need a healer, Wistler."

Another maid rushes to the oak table and pours me some fresh water. Shyly, she helps steady my hand when my tremor almost causes me to spill the water all over the floor. It has been a full day since I last had a drink, and the water tastes crisp and refreshing, the fruit that has been infused offering a freshness that I savour.

"Still, it would not hurt for a healer to cast their eyes over you. It would be wise for you to accept help every once in a while." Wistler saunters over and passes me some bread which I gladly take from him. "Now, how is it that you come to be in my hall, sat on my throne, in the state that you are in?" There is growl in his voice that tells me he is not happy. I smile at him. Perhaps he does have a little fight in him after all.

"Uster has fallen, Wistler." I take a bite out of the warm

bread, the smell of wheat drifting up my nose as I inhale. Bread has never smelt so good.

"What do you mean, *fallen*?"

"It lies in ruins, near enough burnt to the ground. It was a smouldering ruin when I arrived. The villagers and soldiers based there have been slaughtered." My mind traces over my conversation with the dying guard I found. The stench of blood and ash are still present on my clothes.

"Who – who did this?" Wistler asks, paling.

"It was the Barbaraqs." I take a large bite of my bread and chew it as though I have no inclination towards proper etiquette anymore. The satisfaction of ending the chieftain's life – the savage who killed my father and my sister – is still fresh in my mind.

"The Barbaraqs have not been seen on our lands for near twenty years. Why after all this time would they suddenly be here? And why would they burn the port of Uster to the ground?"

"The Wyverns." My mouth is still filled with bread as I speak, so I quickly swallow it and wash it down with some water. "Do not fear though, Wistler. Despite their numbers, I challenged the Barbaraq chieftain." I cut Wistler a wry smile. "And he now greets the afterlife."

If possible, Wister's skin becomes almost translucent as he staggers back away from me. "The Barbaraqs are savages, Morgana. If you have slain the chieftain, a challenge will take place for someone to step into his place. They will likely want vengeance. The Barbaraqs value blood as payment for debts owed to them!"

"Let them come. We will meet them at the gates and send them to join their leader."

"This is madness, Morgana." Wistler's cheeks regain

some colour as his features change from panic to anger. "They will arrive at the gates with nothing in mind other than bloodshed. They will slaughter everyone. Eltera will fall! We simply do not have the soldiers to sustain an attack."

"They have seen what I can do with my magic. If they have any sense, they will stay their weapons and keep their distance from Eltera." But privately, I know Wistler is right about one thing: they will come, and they will demand my head.

"We can't possibly defend ourselves!"

"Must I plan everything, Wistler? The Wyverns conspire with the Barbaraqs. If they do attack, we need the people of Eltera to help us."

"And how in the blazes do you plan on coordinating that?" Spittle leaves Wistler's exasperated mouth. It is not like he has anything better to suggest. He would simply roll over and let the people of this kingdom fall with no effort to fight back.

"I will send word to Orjan and Sparrow to warn them of the impending attack. Maybe they will be able to bring the people of Eltera to arms. We will provide them with armour and weapons."

"And what if they turn on us, what if they attempt to storm this castle as they did after the witch trials?" Wistler's face is scarlet with rage.

I stand from my chair, straightening my bodice as I do so. "Either we fight, or Eltera falls, and that is something that I cannot allow. The King's War depends on it."

And so does my ascent to the throne.

28

ORJAN

"*The Barbaraq's traditionally wield weapons such as axe's and hatchets, attacking with a fierceness unrivalled by many. Slaughtering the men in any town or village in which they pillage, taking the women to claim as their wives and the children to raise as their own.*"

Gleya Frederich, Levanthria, A History, 212KR

A KNOCK at the door startles me from my sleep, and I drag myself up into a sitting position, the heat of the sun landing on my face through the window.

"Who is it?"

"It's me, Sparrow. Can I come in?"

"You may." For a moment I am reminded of my life as a knight, when I still had prestige and lived in my manor in luxury, with my every wish tended to by the maids. For once, it is a welcome memory.

Now it just feels like a luxury to have slept in a real bed, rickety as it is. The innkeeper showed me a kindness in allowing me to stay in one of his rooms at no charge.

Despite it being cramped, I am thankful for the gesture and for once I have woken with only a mild headache from the previous night's antics.

Sparrow slips into the room, closing the door behind her.

"Come," she whispers. "We have to move quickly. Heath has begun to pull everyone from the rebellion together. He has called an urgent meeting to discuss matters. We need to introduce you and explain that you are on our side, that we want the same thing. The end of the Wyverns."

"And Breyton's head," I add.

Sparrow nods, then spins on her heels and heads off down the corridor.

She is a wise woman, and a better person than she realises. For her to forgive me for what I have done to her husband, to absolve me of the guilt that burrows deep into my skin, is something I will be forever grateful for. It is a kindness that I do not deserve.

I follow Sparrow downstairs to find a group of people in the midst of what appears to be a heated disagreement.

"Order!" a man bellows amongst the impassioned arguments. "Need I remind you what will happen should the Wyverns know we are here?"

I duck my head under the doorframe as I enter behind Sparrow, and the room falls deadly silent. I immediately spot Heath, whose face is still bruised, but the cut above his left eye appears to be healing well. He is of a strong build but seems as though he has lost some weight since our last encounter. His clothes are in a subpar state, with his shirt torn in several places. If I didn't know better, I might think the man possessed no home.

His eyes meet my own and I look away quickly, casting

my eyes downwards as I follow Sparrow to the front of the room while stony gazes seem to burn holes through me.

"Why is he here?" a voice calls from the back of the room.

"He's one of them!"

"He will bring the Wyverns to our door!"

"You have brought the dragon into our house!"

Heath raises one of his hands to draw silence from the hostile crowd, his other hand gripped tightly to the crutch that enables him to stand. A makeshift splint is fastened to the outside of his leg. He grimaces as he pushes himself into a central position in front of the crowd.

"I have brought us all together because my wife, Delaya, vouched for this man. I have brought us all together because we cannot sit by and continue to let the Wyverns govern this kingdom with their self-imposed rules."

The crowd begins to hush one another into silence until eventually only Heath speaks. "I am a proud Elterian. I was born and raised here, and I cannot and will not sit by another day and let them continue to terrorise us. It was a dark day when the fires of the witch trials tore through the markets the way they did. No one could have predicted the Wyverns taking over so quickly, but their numbers far exceeded those of the guards that Lord Wistler employs to keep us safe." Heath speaks powerfully and is a natural speaker, his voice booming over everyone in the room, commanding they listen.

"That coward abandoned us. Left us to rot and suffer in squalor. He is as bad as them lot out there!" a scrawny young man yells, and a few heads nod in agreement.

"Aye, he did. Lord Wistler is not innocent in all of this, but he will have done what he thought was the best thing to maintain Eltera. After all, the Wyverns have not been able to penetrate the castle walls."

Some of the crowd jeer Heath for his defence of their lord in hiding.

"He should have done more to protect us," the scrawny man continues, elevating his voice. "I say when we take back the streets from the Wyverns, we take the castle too." The crowd begins to rally behind him with enthused approval.

"How are we supposed to take back the streets?" one woman demands. "We've never been able to before."

"For too long have we met in secret while the Wyverns do as they wish with us. We have bided our time for a moment, for a sign. I say that today is the day that we take back our kingdom, that we spit in the faces of the Wyverns and we tell them no more! We have a man on the inside that wants to help us, that wants to end the Wyverns' reign, that wants to bring Breyton to justice. We have Orjan!"

"That is not a man, he is a beast! There is a reason why they call him the dragon!" the scrawny man continues in opposition to Heath.

Heath's face grows exasperated. "His name is Orjan, and he is a knight of Rashouya. He is honour bound."

The crowd continues to heckle, and I realise I have no option other than to speak up for myself.

"If I may," I interrupt, stepping forward. The scrawny man suddenly doesn't look so confident now that he is in such close proximity to my scaled skin. "I am ashamed of my actions, of the things I have done. Not just in Eltera but in Askela, Voraz, Treventine. I know I have caused harm and fear to the people of this kingdom, and for that, I am sorry. I will not apologise for doing what I must in order to protect the life of a young boy and his keeper. My name is Orjan, and I was once a knight of Rashouya. Not a dragon, not a beast, but a man of honour."

"Orjan speaks of Rior, the young boy that helps at the shelter who fell onto the wrong side of the Wyverns. They killed one of his keepers and threatened to do the same to him," Sparrow explains to the crowd.

"Bollocks!" a voice calls out.

"She speaks the truth," I answer back. "Trovell and his goons told me that if I fought in the pits, they would keep away from Rior, that no harm would come to him or Preya. Once I agreed to that, they told me to do more, or they would kill the boy. I had no option but to do what they said. I need to get to Breyton, so that I can end this. So that I can end him." If I can keep to my word to Morgana, maybe, just maybe, I will have regained a little bit of honour. Her promise to help find a cure for my curse bubbles up inside of me, but I push it away, not wanting to succumb to futile hope. Right now, I need to focus on protecting the people of Eltera.

"Orjan is one of us," Heath says with finality. "When the time is right, he will lead us into battle against our enemy. Are you with us?"

A raucous cheer comes from the crowd, and it hits me in the chest like a battering ram. For too long have people spat at me for simply walking past, recoiled in horror at my appearance whilst calling me all manner of names. The fact that these people cheer for me stirs something within me that I have not felt for some time. These people have trust in me, for some reason. Despite everything that I have done, they cheer my name. They offer willingly to go into battle with me, to fight by my side as we seek to liberate them from the tyranny of the Wyverns.

There is a sudden bang on the door and the room falls into a state of instant anxiety.

"Is it them, do they know we are here?" someone in the crowd asks.

"Hush," Heath demands as he casts a nod towards the innkeeper.

Petor moves to the door and opens it slightly. After a moment that feels like a lifetime of apprehension, he allows a young maid to enter.

"Says she has a message for Sparrow and Orjan. From Morgana."

The anxiety lifts in the room but I can't help but wonder what would cause Morgana to risk sending a message to us in broad daylight.

"Morgana is in need of help from you and the people of Eltera. The Barbaraqs have made shore on Levanthrian land, and they march to our gates as we speak. Lord Wistler does not have enough guards to ensure that we survive an attack. She seeks help from the people of Eltera to fight alongside her and the guards to see that Eltera does not fall victim to their savagery."

The room falls into chaotic talk in an instant.

"How long do we have?" Heath asks.

"Half a day at most," the maid says, trembling as she speaks.

"Then we need to make haste." Heath turns to address the room. "Ready yourselves with anything that will pass as a weapon."

My heart sinks. We barely have the weapons we need to reclaim the streets from within, let alone arm ourselves against a citywide assault.

"There's more," the maid interrupts. "Lady Morgana has

stated that if you head to the castle, she will arm you with what weapons they have to spare."

As a flurry of motion and chatter breaks out in the room, I realise that we might be the only ones aware of the impending attack. I head to the door, where Sparrow attempts to intercept me.

"Where is it you go?" she asks.

"I need to warn Rior and Preya. Then I will go and see Trovell, they need to know about this. We're going to need the Wyverns in this fight, for better or for worse," I add at the look of uncertainty on her face. "When this over, we'll rid ourselves of them once and for all."

But in this moment, it is not our fight against the Wyverns that grips me. The Barbaraqs destroyed my life all those years ago, and now here they are, at my doorstep.

I intend to take my revenge.

29

ORJAN

W hen I enter the shelter, I sense an eery quietness about the place. No one sits in wait for food and water as I have been accustomed to seeing when I arrive. Empty makeshift chairs line either side of the room and the counter is unmanned.

"Rior!" I call. "Preya!" Nothing greets me but the echoes of my own voice. Where in the blazes could they be? The place is usually buzzing with people at this time of the morning as Rior helps serve breakfast to the needy.

I poke my head through the door into the kitchen, but inside, I find no smell of freshly baked bread, no warmth from the ovens. When I walk through to make my way to the stairs at the far side of the room, I notice a tray on the floor, and a couple of pans. I move towards them and kneel to pick them up. At the base of one of the pans I find blood, as if the pan were used to hit someone.

My heart sinks. Have the Wyverns gone back on their word? If they have harmed Rior in any way, I will never forgive myself.

My anger rising, I race back to the library, the harsh sun

and dry air stinging my throat with each breath I take. My rasping grumbles warn everyone in my vicinity that I am not in the best of moods. My chest pounds, my head throbs, and my blood boils as my thoughts get the better of me. I run through countless scenarios of the unspeakable things Grush and his men could have done to Rior or Preya.

I need to find them, and fast. The crowds are picking up as I near the markets and the hustle and bustle of the people of Eltera becomes somewhat of an inconvenience. I walk as if I see no one, barging past people who think twice on cursing me. They know my reputation. They know what I am capable of. One or two faces that I catch, I recognise from the meeting just a short while ago. They are going about their duties and speaking to people in small groups, gathering supplies for the impending attack. The timing of Rior and Preya's disappearance could not have come at a worse time.

People stop and whisper as I rush through, my face stony, my eyes wide with anger. The old library ahead has two Wyverns standing at the front, smoking pipes and pushing one another.

It takes everything I have not to rip their throats out as I storm into the entrance. Inside, the smell of stale ale barely masks the stench of fresh blood, and I pray it's not Rior's or Preya's. Dishevelled men and women are inside the pit clearing up the mess from the night before. One of the cleaners looks completely desensitised to the thick blood she mops in the centre of the pit. When they see me storming through, they all stop in their tracks, following my steps as I charge towards Trovell's office in the back.

I lunge forward and plant my boot on his door, already drawing my own conclusions.

"Where the fuck is the boy!" I bellow as the door splinters, falling from its hinges.

"The blazes is this?" Trovell sits at his desk, quill in hand. His eyes flicker with panic when he sees the rage etched across my face. I rush at him, wrapping my right hand around his throat and slamming him into the wall.

Trovell wraps his hands around my forearm and desperately gasps for air as I push him up against the wall, into the air until his feet leave the floor.

"Where is Rior? Where is Preya?" I growl. "We had a deal that no harm would come to them!"

"That was before you were seen leaving a rebel meeting." Grush's gravelled voice sends my blood boiling further. I glance over my shoulder to see him and a handful of his men entering the room. It is an enclosed space, making it difficult to fight, but I am past caring at this point. I hurl Trovell towards Grush and he bounces into one of the entering henchmen. Trovell lets out a groan and begins coughing as he desperately gasps for air. Two men rush towards me, but I crash my shoulder into one of them before slamming my fist into the other's chest. His bones crack loudly under the force, and he writhes around on the floor like the snake that he is. Another Wyvern reaches me this time with a wooden plank in his hand. He raps it over my head with a dull thud, and it snaps in two from the impact. The colour drains from the Wyvern responsible and I grab hold of him by the scruff of his neck, slamming him through Trovell's desk. Rolls of parchment are flattened in an instant as dust and ink spray into the air.

I breathe deeply, advancing on Grush, who simply grins at me in return as he stoops down to help Trovell up from the floor. Trovell slips out of the room, but Grush remains, and I shove his face into the wall.

"Where is the boy? I will not ask again."

"I was right about you. Trovell was a fucking fool to trust you!" Grush says. "Trust me when I say I am going to have fun with the boy and his keeper. That is, if they have survived the last hour with my men."

My blood runs cold. My anger consumes me and I lose what little control remains. I dive forward into Grush and plant my head into his mouth. The two of us fall through the door, taking out a section of the doorframe. I pin Grush down and draw my fist back, taking in his smiling, bloodied face. I bring my fist down on him again and again. Grush simply laughs at me.

"Now!" he spits, his blood spraying over me as I pull back my fist once more.

Something heavy wraps around me and drags me to my side. I try to stand but it is difficult to move. It takes a few seconds for me to realise I have been hit with some form of metal netting. I struggle to move, the weight of the net making it increasingly difficult as my limbs get tangled up. Grush rolls onto his side and spits a mouthful of blood onto the floor beside him before staring me in the eyes.

"Fell into that one, didn't you?" he sneers as he brings himself back to his feet. He slams his boot into my head over and over again until I find it hard to focus on anything in the room. Grush blurs into our surroundings as I barely hold onto consciousness.

The ground begins to move underneath me as his men drag me. I feel like a trapped animal, and should they remove this constraint, they will see me act like one. I find myself bouncing off the stone steps to the base of the pit, the hardened shell on my back taking the brunt of the force until I come to a halt in the dirt.

"If you want to see Rior alive, I suggest you keep still,"

Grush demands as he lifts the mesh from over the top of my head. "Now stand up!"

With no option but to comply, I reluctantly stand, my breath laboured as I attempt to suppress my anger. Grush pushes me backwards until I hit the edge of the pit. His men are on me at once, and I am chained to the wall. Once I am secured, the Wyverns quickly jump back away from me.

I pull against the chains, but I am fixed to the spot. I can only imagine what Grush has in store for me, his grin wild with anticipation.

The Wyverns start to gather around the edge of the pit as they jeer and heckle me. Some of them are still smarting from their injuries that I have just inflicted on them. They want to see my blood spill, they want to see me fall. They grow more raucous as I struggle against my constraints, shouting profanities about each and every way that they would like to see me suffer.

"You will pay for your insolence!" Trovell shrieks from the top of the steps, his hand pressed against his red, raw neck. Streaks of blood run down where my claw-like nails pierced his skin. He pants heavily as he dead-stares me from a safe distance. I do not flinch nor cower, and I stare straight back at him in an act of defiance.

"If you are so sure of this, why don't you step into this pit with me?" I goad him.

"Breyton will have your head for this!"

I find it hard to believe that the man even exists, having never laid eyes on him since landing in Eltera.

Trovell raises his hand and the Wyverns fall silent as he addresses them. "This beast seeks to collude with the rebels that threaten to end our reign. Do these ungrateful parasites not understand what we have done for them since the witch trials that nearly destroyed our city? We have brought order amongst the chaos, and this is the gratitude we get. This monster came to us with an offer. We agreed to the deal, so imagine my shock when this beast bursts into my office and attacks me."

The crowd livens up once more as Trovell paces across the top of the steps to the pit.

"Not only this, but he has the audacity to partake in a meeting with the rebellion. The dragon himself said of his intent to assassinate Breyton, our noble leader!"

The jeering Wyverns begin spitting and jeering once more as they voice their displeasure. It is an approach I have become accustomed too, but I care not for the reaction of the crowd, for now my mind is racing with concern for Rior and Preya.

"He went against our deal! What do you think we should do?"

The crowd erupts, baying for blood to be spilt.

"Grush!" I roar. "We do not have time for this, there is an enemy bearing –"

Grush interrupts me by gesturing with his hands and what I see causes my words to stick in my throat like a lump of earth.

Grush smiles as two of his thugs step forward with Rior and Preya in front of them. With a shove, the two of them roll down the stairs into the pit, much to the laughter of the watching Wyverns. Rior's left eye is swollen shut and his torn shirt reveals grazes below his collarbone. Preya looks just as bad, if not worse. Her nose sits crooked on her face above a split lip, and cuts and grazes shine through her ripped dress all over her arms.

What I wouldn't give to be in these pits alone with only Grush for company.

Trovell raises his hands once more, drawing silence from

the spectators revelling in the show that unfolds before them. "Now, as I said, we had a deal with the dragon. We would bring forward sacrifices as they are, people who had committed crimes against the Wyverns. He would then choose which ones would live and which ones would die." His eyes sparkle as he whips the crowd up into a frenzy.

I can already see what is coming; the bastard wants me to pick one of them to live.

"I will not do it!" I roar. "I will not choose!"

"I thought you might say that," Trovell sneers as he passes a dagger to Grush.

Grush takes the knife and juggles it from one hand to the other as he descends the steps into the pit.

"If you touch them, I will kill you!" I pull against my constraints as hard as I can, willing the bolts that hold them in place to come loose. The rattle of the chains only seems to rile up the crowd even more as Grush draws level with Rior and Preya.

My head drops. I can't bear to see the pain in their eyes. "I am sorry!"

A metallic chime rings, which causes me to lift my head. Grush has dropped a dagger in between the two of them. "One of you will die today. If he won't choose, one of you will have to." Grush's twisted gaze moves from Rior to Preya, then to me as he unsheathes a larger dagger from his belt. This one has serrated edges like a saw.

He intends to torture me. But my skin is far thicker than it used to be, the scales giving it leather-like protection.

"I have been studying you, Dragon, and I think I know where your weakness lies. Aside from that cold heart of yours." Grush moves to my side and rams the blade into the gap between my back and my hardened shell. It crunches, as if he's breaking open a clam shell. My eyes widen as a searing pain burns down my side. My legs begin to shake as I stare down at the ground, watching as my own blood splashes around my feet, converging with the dirt on the ground.

"Stop! You can't do this!"

I snap my head back and stare at Rior. "Whatever they do to me, do not do anything. If there is blood to be spilled in this pit today, it is mine."

"But Orjan –" Rior's face is wet with tears.

Before I have a chance to say anything, Grush drags the dagger upwards, hacking through my skin. I feel every inch of the tear widening, the fibres of my skin ripping slowly. Blood warms the back of my legs as Grush takes his time running his blade across me until he eventually stands on the opposite side of me. The pain is excruciating, and it is all I can do to clench my jaw tightly to suppress my agony. My whole body shakes and my back feels as though it is on fire. Despite the agony, I do not give Grush the satisfaction of my screams.

Grush grunts with the effort it requires to cut through my cursed skin. As he reaches the bottom of my back, I pray to the gods that this will soon be over. He presses the pain in deeper and the sharp sting worsens as though it is a red-hot poker that Grush wields and not a knife.

As Grush reaches his starting point, I cling onto consciousness, surrounded by my thick, crimson blood. Through the cheers of the crowd, I can hear the screamed protests of Rior and Preya, but my vision is too blurred to see them.

I fall forward, my arms pulled behind me by my suspended chains. Here I hang limply, unable to bear my own weight. I am too weak, I am losing too much blood. Grush begins tampering with my chains, and suddenly my arms become free and I fall onto my knees. I just about manage to stop myself face-planting in the dirt, panting heavily as I fight back against the worsening pain. I do not know how much longer I can hold on.

"I am not done yet, Dragon." Grush laughs before kicking me forward. My face smashes into the ground and in that instant, a flash of light takes over my vision. I swear for a moment I see stars as my pointed jaw smashes into the roof of my mouth, my lip tearing as my jagged teeth pierce my skin. The taste of iron is one that I haven't experienced in a long time.

I try to fight back, to push through. I gather as much strength as I can muster and press myself up from the floor.

"Get up, Orjan, you have to get up!" Rior's cries punch through the raucous cheers of the crowd and I try my hardest to focus on his words. To use them to motivate me. My arms, however, have other ideas, and they give way, causing my face to meet the dirt once again.

"You're pathetic!" Grush sneers as he grips the scruff of my tunic from behind. "I am going to show our people that it is possible to tear you apart."

A sudden pressure bears down on me as he begins to rip my hardened shell from my back. The further ripping of my skin is agonising, pain like I have never experienced, making being hacked at with a dagger pale in comparison.

"Stop, please, you're killing him!" Rior's pained shrieks make this torture even more unbearable.

I again try to push myself up from the mud, but I have no fight in me. My back sears as if molten rock has been poured over my skin. Grush continues to force back the shell and I can hear the sound of my own flesh tearing. I can hold it in no longer, and I roar out as abject agony takes over my body. I begin to convulse from the pain, hearing every grunt and snort from Grush as he continues to peel my shell off my back, my arms and body wet with thick, coursing blood.

Then the weight lifts as broad cheers from above reach their crescendo. With a crack and a snap, my shell is torn from my back. It feels as though a bone has been broken, a huge weight lifted from me, but I feel exposed. A coldness washes over my back like nothing I have felt before. The dizziness becomes all-consuming as my loss of blood is bringing me ever closer to death. The noise around me becomes muffled as the blurred outline of Grush wanders past me, raising my shell like a trophy for all to see. Given how much he hates me, I fully expect him to mount it on a wall to show how he slayed the dragon that ravaged Eltera. He chucks my shell to one side and turns in my direction, removing his serrated dagger from his waist as he approaches me.

I welcome death. I welcome a release from the torture that I have endured far longer than the sickening show being put on now.

"He's had enough, you're going to kill him!" Preya shouts in anguish. Rior sobs inconsolably opposite her. No child should witness the things that he has.

"One of you has to die. Trovell demands it, Breyton demands it." Grush continues his slow walk to me as though he is biding his time.

"Kill me." The words fall from my lips, broken.

Preya rushes for the dagger on the ground, and I pray she does this to end my suffering, to bury that dagger into my skull and put me out of my misery. She stumbles to her feet, gripping the dagger in both of her hands.

I raise my head and look her in the eyes as best as I can, barely gripping onto consciousness. "Please." The hissed word escapes my lips. "It's all right. Do it." An end to my pain is all I wish for in this moment. At least if I die, Rior and Preya will be free. My life for theirs.

Preya raises the dagger high into the air and I brace myself for the blow, ready.

"You promised you would look after Rior," she says, her voice trembling. "Make sure you do." Then she plunges the dagger into her stomach. The crowd cheers once more, and I wish in this moment that I had the strength to tear out the throats of each and every one of the sick bastards.

"Preya!" Rior screams and rushes towards her, sliding onto his knees and cradling her head in his arms. She takes her last breath as Rior presses his forehead into hers, sobbing.

The doors swing open, followed by the echoed sound of boots. Rior's muffled cry is suddenly all that remains as he begs and pleads for Preya to wake. There is only one person I can think of that holds the power to draw instant silence from these animals.

Breyton.

30

MORGANA

"It is prophesied that on a day that the thirteen moons align, magical energy will be released into this world by the gods like nothing seen before. That this power will bring about it the end of these worlds. Mark my words, I believe that the day of the Zagruist will come, it is only a matter of when."

Unknown, Journal entry, 05KR

I SCRATCH my quill frantically against the parchment with trembling hands as I write. I cannot allow Eltera to fall, and I fear that we do not have enough to stop the impending assault from the Barbaraqs. My words are written in haste but with a clear message to Codrin back in Askela: send reinforcements at once.

I place the letter into an envelope, then press a wax seal using Jareb's ring. The hot wax stings against my skin, but I find the burning sensation soothing, and I hold my hand to the wax longer than needed.

"You sent for me." Dante's words startle me from my stupor.

"I need you to ride to Askela and deliver this message to Codrin," I tell him, passing him the letter. "I must ask that you set off at haste and do not delay."

Dante's blue eyes search over me, the creases on his weary face intensifying. "Lady Morgana, I must protest. If the Barbaraqs are to assault Eltera as we suspect, I will be needed here. Would you not be best sending a messenger boy or one of your maids to send for help?" Dante is as bloodied and exhausted as myself. We have been awake for far longer than our bodies should naturally allow, and his face is still sprayed with the blood of his fallen comrades. The ones who followed me to death. Purple bags have formed under his drooping eyes, and judging by his swaying, I imagine it is only adrenaline that keeps him from collapsing before me.

I place my palms over one of his hands, his skin rough and warm to the touch. He lets his hands rest between mine tentatively, as though he does not trust me. I do not blame him; I have given him little reason to, especially after leading his comrades to their early graves.

"You followed me without hesitation or question, Dante. That kind of loyalty is rare in this world. This message is important. We need help if we are to save this city. I need someone who can defend themselves across the plains, I need someone who can ride quickly. If we can keep the Barbaraqs at bay for long enough, Codrin might just be able to get to us in time."

"And if he doesn't?" Dante's hand trembles between my own, and I can feel his pulsating blood like a rhythmic song. Our eyes meet and I channel some of my energy to replenish his own. His ailment is fatigue, and as such, it takes little of my power to rejuvenate him. A heat generates between my hands, and I watch as the gauntness in his face subsides, the bags under his eyes fading as if he had the best night's sleep of his life.

"Then he will avenge this fallen kingdom. There. You should feel fine to ride now." I let go of his hand.

Dante brings his hand up and stares at it in disbelief, "Th – thank you. I will ride straight away."

"Do not stop. Get that message to Codrin as fast as you can."

"What will you do in the meantime?" Dante asks as the two of us quickly make our way towards the courtyard where his horse stands in wait. To my alarm, I see no urgency from the guards. They go about their tasks as if today is just a normal day in Eltera.

"What is this!" I demand. Has Wistler not conveyed my message? Why is it that he has taken no action to prepare the guards for the Barbaraqs?

Dante mounts his steed before casting me one last glance. I slap the horse on the rear and Dante sets off at pace, almost taking out a burly man who carries a large bowl full of grain.

I search the courtyard, but Wistler is nowhere to be seen. I grab the arm of a passing guard and spin him to speak to me. "Where is Wistler?"

"I – I don't know." The guard cowers as if he fears I will end his life.

"Have you been briefed?" I ask, my voice elevating as my frustration rises. The man casts a confused expression over me as if the words I mumble are that of a madwoman. "Tell me, have you been briefed on the impending attack by the Barbaraqs?"

The guard merely returns a blank expression. What

games is it that Wistler plays? No doubt he is hiding under a rock somewhere, quaking with fear. The man has no spine, and every inch of him shows cowardice I have never seen before.

"Prepare to defend Eltera," I say, raising my voice for all to hear. "The Barbaraqs are on their way. Every man, woman, and child in the city that is able to must take up arms."

The guard continues to stare at me as if frozen under some sort of spell.

"Now!" I order. The man moves and begins shouting orders at the rest of the guards, who, although confused by my commands, do not hesitate to move into action.

"'Scuse me."

I feel a tug at the back of my dress and turn to face a little girl. She wears the stained uniform of the scullery maids, rubbing her fingers against the fabric nervously.

"What is it?" I do not have time for idle chat.

The girl averts her gaze, intimidated my tone. "It . . . it's Lord Wistler, miss," she stammers. "I know where it is he went."

The girl has my attention. I want to know where the pig is so I can skin him myself. "Go on." I smile and the girl loosens her grip on her tunic.

"He headed into the markets. I heard him say that's where he was going."

"That is all." I dismiss the girl and make for the gates into Eltera. If I need to drag him back here to fight alongside the others, I will. If he won't, I will see to it that everyone witnesses his execution.

As I reach the streets of Eltera, I am passed by a swathe of men and woman making their way towards the castle gates. This reassures me that my message to Orjan and

Sparrow has been received. Something does not seem right, however. The more I look, the less I see of the Wyverns. Where they would normally be loitering on every street corner, harassing people in the streets, there is nothing. More people knock into me as they make their way past, and I hear murmurings and whispers of my warning being heeded by the common folk.

At least they have heeded my warning, which is more than I can say for Wistler. There is no sign of him as I patrol the streets, and I do not have long to find him before I will need to return to the castle walls to ensure that the guards are setting up the correct defensive formations. When I attacked the Barbaraq camp, I saw no signs of siege equipment, so how is it they intend to storm the walls?

Roaring cheers and shouting at the western side of the markets snaps me back to attention. I follow the sounds until I am led to the entranceway of what looks like an old library. This must be where the pits are that Orjan told me about. Judging by the blood, vomit, and tankards scattered on the ground around me, this is no longer used for its former purpose. The smell of stale ale wafts into my face and hits me like a wet cloth, the musty smell unforgiving. The rapturous noise continues inside with men and woman chanting and cheering as if they are singing bards.

"Breyton, Breyton, Breyton!"

My heart races. The bastard is here. The man responsible for my being here is just beyond these doors.

There are far too many Wyverns here for me to dispatch on my own. All I need is to get close enough to Breyton. Close enough to snuff out his life just like I did the Barbaraq chieftain. I pull my hood up and step inside, sliding into the shadows beside the doorway. Maybe I can get a clear shot of

Breyton and hit him with a blast of energy from where I stand.

Standing at the far side of the library overlooking a large hole in the ground, a hooded figure raises his hands to draw silence from his people. So this is the man responsible for the downfall of Eltera.

As silence falls over the room, I hear the sobs of a child, but I am not sure where the sound comes from.

"Preya! Preya, come back, wake up, please wake up."

Breyton stands at the head of the pit, casting his eyes down upon whoever is unlucky enough to be in there. His wears a dark purple tunic with gilded edges, which gives the mark of someone who enjoys the finer luxuries in life, unlike the rest of the people he presides over.

"Let it be seen that this is what happens to those that cross the Wyverns."

My eyes widen as Breyton speaks, for I recognise his voice in an instant. He begins to lower his hood, freeing his face from the shadows.

"Wistler." I hiss his name, drawing the brief attention of several bystanders. For now, everyone's eyes remain fixed on their leader. If I wanted to gut the man like a pig before, now I want to drag him through the streets of Eltera by his entrails. My heart beats faster as my anger rises. The coward was behind this the whole time. And I had no idea.

"Let me take in the beast before you, let me see the one you call Dragon." Wistler moves to the top step of the pit and looks down. His face lights up as he takes in whatever spectacle lies in there. The crowd cheers.

"This beast thought he could double-cross us, thought he could help the people of this wretched kingdom rise up," Wistler sneers, his face venomous with rage. "Look at him now, look at where his futile attempt at regaining some semblance of honour has gotten him. Facedown and in the dirt, his armoured shell torn from his back."

In this moment I know that my plan has failed, and my panic flares. Orjan is dead at the hands of the Wyverns. Is this what will trigger Laith to kill me when he hears of it? What if Laith were to discover that it was I who sent Orjan here to infiltrate the Wyverns, and as such, cost him his life? The hatred that Laith has in his eyes as he kicks me over the edge to my death is one that only grief can bring.

By trying to evade my fate, I may have merely brought it to my doorstep.

I feel a twinge of regret for Orjan's demise. I had high hopes that he would ring true to his task and bring an end to Breyton's reign of terror, but like so many others before him, he has let me down.

I edge closer through the crowd until I can make out the scene below: a boy, crying over a slaughtered woman. And Orjan.

Alive. But barely.

In this moment, I realise I must do everything I can to save him. He is the key, after all. If I can keep him alive, I might still be able to deter my fate. But there are too many Wyverns here, and my magic stores are still depleted after fighting the Barbaraq chieftain. I have to get Breyton alone. Or come back after I've chosen a victim to replenish myself.

"As planned, the Barbaraqs are on their way," Wistler continues as I turn to leave. "My offer of allegiance has been accepted by their chieftain. We will march to the gates and let them in."

I stop dead in my tracks as icy shock consumes me.

Wistler paces back and forth at the top of the pit. "They know not to target Wyverns, so make sure your properties and armour are painted with our colours. Everything else is theirs to pillage as they see fit. Treasures, women, children."

Why? Why would Wistler commit such an atrocity? Why would he allow the savages in? They will slaughter everyone they set upon.

"The Barbaraqs' numbers swell. They are a growing force to be reckoned with. With them by our side, I have no doubt that we will be powerful enough to storm Askela, to take back rule over Levanthria. King Athos Almerion has been absent for years! It is about time we took back control of our lands."

"What of the sorceress?" a voice calls out from the crowd.

"Yeah, she won't allow this to happen. She acts on the king's behalf."

Wistler has a confident swagger about him which I am not used to seeing. "Leave Morgana to me. She will not survive this night. True, her arrival and insistence on staying has not been ideal, and she has been a thorn in my side. Despite the magic, she will not be able to overcome our combined numbers."

I can't help but smile at his insolence. His words simply add fuel to my burning anger. How little the man knows me. I have never run from a fight. I head into every battle knowing full well that the gods favour me. This is not the night that I will greet the afterlife.

A spark of magic ignites in my hand, the static sensation causing the hairs on my arms to stand on end. I let my energy surge up my arm and around my body, feeling exhilarated.

"Breyton!" An older man in fine dark robes limps to Breyton's side, his frailties telling me that like Breyton, he is used to having others do his bidding. "Our scouts send word that the Barbaraqs are approaching the gates."

"Paint the sign of the Wyverns on your walls and your armour! Head to the gates and ready yourselves. Tonight, the Wyverns rise up. Tonight, the Wyverns take over the whole of Eltera. Then Levanthria!" Wistler pumps his fist into the air and the Wyverns set about to some barrels at the side of the rooms. They splash their hands inside and begin smearing red paint over their chests as directed.

"Wistler!" I bellow. Moving out of the shadows, I plant my palm into the face of a scrawny Wyvern beside me and bed my fingers into his skin. Within a moment I am channelling his life force to replenish my own. I have no desire for discretion anymore as my anger at Wistler's treachery consumes me. The magic courses through my hand and down to my free arm and I stare straight into Wistler's unforgiving eyes. It is as though he does not fear me, as if a different person stands before me, someone far braver. The pressure in my hand grows until I release a bolt of magic at him.

He grabs hold of the older man and yanks him in front of himself. My magic hits the man in the chest, and he collapses aggressively to the floor, his life snuffed out in an instant.

"To the gates!" Wistler commands. He makes smug eye contact with me from across the room, then disappears into the crowd. Many of the Wyverns follow him, but a few are stupid enough to remain behind. Clenching my fists, I begin to summon the dark magic that I can wield, drawing all the shadows in the room to my palms. A dark energy emits from my body, causing the dust on the ground to rise up and whip around me as if I am the centre of a storm.

The crowd screams as the Wyverns push and shove each

other in the small space, scrambling to retreat. I fire out a
blast of energy that obliterates the room in an instant,
sending bodies hurtling across the room. Books come
crashing down from the walls, torn pages whipping into the
air as though a tornado has breached the walls. As I walk
towards the pit, groans of the Wyverns that remain
conscious capture my attention, and one of them tries in
vain to crawl to safety. I stretch out my arm and drain him of
his life force, then point towards the others in the room and
do the same to them, replenishing the magic I have just
used. Faces become taut and aged, withering away until
nothing but bones and dust remain. The burning sensation
crippling my body subsides, replaced by a warmth that
soothes me. I rush down the steps and into the pit where the
young boy kneels in terror, cradling the head of a dead
woman. He cowers in terror as I near him. Then my attention is drawn to Orjan who lies motionless, surrounded by
pool of his crimson blood with his face buried in the dirt.
His hardened shell has been torn from his back, and his
skin hangs loosely from its edges.

I might be too late.

I kneel, placing my hands upon him as I summon my
magic. Energy begins coursing through him from my fingertips, my hands pulsating to a euphoric, heartbeat-like
rhythm.

Orjan's heart stops. My intervention has come too late,
his soul is now in the afterlife and my fate is sealed.

"No," I whisper. "No!" I channel my magic harder, even
as the euphoria morphs into pain. He cannot die on this
night. His death will all but confirm the vision I have seen.
And on top of that, I have an alternative reason that
surprises even myself: I don't want Orjan to die.

Orjan convulses as his body pushes back against my

magic. What I am doing is not natural. Bringing someone back from the brink of death is like wading into the afterlife and telling the gods to go fuck themselves. Agonising pain sears my arms, and my veins begin to protrude from my skin as if they are ready to burst. A stabbing sensation rips through my back and I know my magic is working as I begin to absorb some of Orjan's injuries into my own body. I can't take it all, however; to do so would end my life too.

I absorb what I can, and Orjan's wounded back begins to heal and scar before my eyes. The hidden force between us becomes unmanageable, and my arms are forced back away from him. I shriek in pain as my wrist snaps back. The connection to my magic breaks and I collapse on the floor beside him, writhing in pain from using the darkest of forbidden magic. It has been years since I let my magic course through my own body, always relying on the life force of others.

The young boy's eyes are wide with fear at the spectacle as I reach my hand towards him, in need of replenishing. It is as though hot knives take it in turns to stab through every inch of my skin as my magic use takes its toll. My veins burn but my body shivers. I know he is only a boy, but I need to stop this pain before it destroys me.

The boy sits frozen in terror as I place my hands on the sides of his face.

31

ORJAN

I am somehow conscious. My body is broken, my mind tortured. If the gods were to show any level of kindness, they would end my miserable existence in this moment. They would let me close my eyes one last time and drift into the void. No matter where I end up in the afterlife, it could be no worse than where I am now. My back feels soaked, my skin cold and damp as searing pain tears into my senses, as if I have been skinned alive. My body trembles from the shock of what I have endured, the temptation to give in becoming more and more alluring.

The sound of anguished cries reach me through my daze, dragging me back from the encroaching darkness.

It is Rior. It is he who cries out in pain. Morgana's body glows, a greenish colour from her magic whipping up a storm around her. Her hand is outstretched, pointing towards Rior who writhes around in agony ahead of her. His face grows gaunt as he fights back.

"Or – Orjan!" he stutters. "Help me, please!" He reaches his arm out towards me, but it falls limp as he starts to lose his battle.

Something ignites within me. I cannot fail, not again, not in this moment. Everything I touch turns to ash, ends up cursed as I am. Not today. I will not allow Rior to fall. I will not allow myself to fail him. Using every ounce of strength I have, I pound my fists into the blood-soaked ground, pushing myself up. My arms buckle and threaten to collapse, and my head throbs as the darkness continues to seduce me into giving in. My mind traces back to all the times I passed out through intoxication, seeking the void of unconsciousness for comfort. This time it is a dark void of life. If I succumb, Rior dies. And I will have failed him, like everyone else before him.

"NO!" I press down as hard as I can. Bringing myself to my feet, I feel lighter than ever before, as though the heaviest of weights has been lifted from me. Blood rushes to my head and the room spins.

Then I stand taller than I have in years.

"Morgana, stop!" I yell. "He is just a boy!" I don't have time to question how I am even still alive. I should be in the afterlife from my injuries, but instead I find myself dragged back from the brink of death.

I slam my hand down onto Morgana to break her connection, and Rior slumps back into Preya's body.

"The pain, it is unbearable!" Morgana grimaces as she pushes herself up from the ground.

I rush to Rior's side, my breath laboured. "Rior, are you okay?"

I am surprised by the speed at which I move, my back no longer burdened by the weight I am used to. I stretch my back into an arch and it cracks loud enough to shock me that it is not my bones breaking. I can breathe freely. My ribs ache and my skin stings from my injuries, but it is bearable.

Rior stirs and his darkened eyes blink as he comes to.

His face is almost translucent, purplish veins visible through his cheeks. Slowly his colour returns, and the boy becomes more alert to his surroundings. "What was that?" he rasps, short of breath as though he has been running.

"Dark magic." I heave myself to my feet and turn to Morgana, my back clicking. "If I ever find that you have used your magic on a child, especially one I am oath-bound to protect, I will kill you myself. Whether that binds me to this curse for life or not."

My back clicks again as I help Rior to his feet. I stand taller than I ever have, my posture no longer stooped, and Rior looks on in awe as I tower over him. His hands are covered in Preya's blood.

"I am sorry, Rior." These are the only words I can seem to muster. The boy has now lost everything that he holds dear. Both his guardians are dead.

Rior gives me a determined look, his eyes red and filled with tears. "Not as sorry as they will be."

As we speak, Morgana staggers past us and begins climbing the stairs, appearing as though she may collapse at any moment. "We have much to do, Orjan. Breyton plans on letting the Barbaraqs storm Eltera. He wants to form an allegiance between them and the Wyverns. We can't let that happen. The Barbaraqs –"

"I know the Barbaraqs well," I tell her, my mind racing to catch up. "I have faced them in the past. We need to move quickly. I have seen the aftermath these savages leave behind."

Morgana stops in her tracks, giving me an odd look. "Tell me, where was it you had contact with them?"

"A village far to the northeast of Levanthria. Come, we must go." I usher Rior forward and make to follow Morgana, but she doesn't move.

"What happened?" she asks.

"The envoy I was leading happened upon the aftermath. We did what we could to save the villagers left behind. I still remember clearly that only a handful of people made it, including one child which I pulled out of a burning home. We can't let this fate befall Eltera, or any other villages in Levanthria. We need to go, now!"

"It can't be," Morgana murmurs, as if speaking to herself. She eyes me up and down in a strange manner, then seems to come back to herself. "I know who Breyton is. If I can kill him, I can end this and send the Barbaraqs back to their ships. Back to the lands from which they hail. Will you fight?"

I consider the ruthless woman standing before me, unable to forgive her for nearly ending Rior's life. Although I believe her to walk a darkened path, I do sense some good in her. Why else would she be here? Why else would she bring me back from death's grip?

"What do you need me to do?" I ask.

"Eltera cannot fall. Levanthria is depending on it." With this, Morgana takes her leave.

"We must go, Rior. We need to find a safe place for you to hide."

He stares into my eyes, his face darkened with bruising and dust. His swollen lip still seeps with blood. "No!" he says. "I will not run or hide. I have just as much right to fight for Eltera as anyone else in this kingdom."

"Rior, you are just a boy. The Barbaraqs are ruthless fighters. There is no honour within their ranks. If they get the chance, they will butcher you on the spot."

"I will fight. If not beside you, then with the others." He is acting on his anger, his grief.

I want him to hide, but I need to respect his wishes. I

kneel beside Preya and remove the knife, wiping the blade against my pants. Turning back to Rior, I pass him the dagger. He is too small to wield a sword, but at least he will be able to defend himself.

"Stay by my side. If I retreat, you retreat. Do you understand?"

Rior looks shaken now that he is holding a weapon in his hand, and the image is one that reminds me of Esara. I have seen the damage it can do to a child's mind when they are forced to take a life at a young age. I do not wish this of Rior, but he may need to take a life if he is to survive this night.

"Do not hesitate, Rior. If one of them comes close enough to you to strike, you bury that dagger as deep into them as you can."

Rior nods and clutches the dagger tightly to his side, his hands trembling.

I walk towards the pool of my own blood and pick up the shell that has been torn from my back. I investigate it for a moment before pushing my arm through a tough spine that runs vertically down the centre.

"What are you doing?" Rior asks.

I remove my arm from the back of the shell and inspect the outside of it. "This shell has shielded me from many an attack from behind. It is hard enough to block knives and blades. It will make a perfect shield." It is a strange sensation, holding something that has been bound to my back for so long. It is weighted, with a raised bumpy surface that has a texture of porous rock. It is rough with slight markings where blades have made contact with it in the past. I have not thought of it like this before, but if not for the shell that had formed on my back, my life could have been ended on many occasions.

I kneel down and run my hand through my curdling blood, which seems somewhat darker than blood usually is. My blood is cursed, after all. I smear my hand over the front of the shell in two lines, one from top to bottom, one from left to right. Pushing my arm back through the spine of the shell, I bring it around in front of me, and I have a sense of comfort knowing that it will continue to protect me in some way.

"This is the markings of my people. They may have banished me, but I am Rashouyan." If not for the Barbaraqs, the path I have had to walk could have been different.

"Come, we must head to the eastern gate." I take each step with vigour as we make our way to freedom from this place. I spit into the soil as I reach the surface. Hopefully this will be the last time I see this damned place.

Outside, the daylight causes me to squint, the heat of the sun a welcome feeling against my scaled skin. For the first time since I received this curse, I relish the fresh air that I breathe, because it means I am alive.

I have something to fight for. And I will not let this kingdom fall.

32

MORGANA

"*M*organa continues to try and lure me into the trap of working for her, I understand in theory how the magical properties within the ironite can be unlocked. Through using a temperature so high that I only know of one forge capable in Eltera. She tries to seduce me with her ways, and I swear whenever the woman is close in my proximity that I endure a sharp pain in my mind accompanied by a high pitched noise. It is at times unbearable and I can't help but feel she has some part to do with it. She wields dark magic and I do not trust her goal, she seeks to serve herself and not the King, not the people of Eltera."

Diary entry of Jonah Viergen, 255KR

MY MIND WHIRLS LIKE A STORM. It was Orjan. It was he who plucked me from my burning home. It is he who I should thank for my life. How can it be that the cursed man I sent to infiltrate the Wyverns, who somehow has a role to play in my death, was my rescuer as a child? Why would the gods do this? Why would they intwine our lives in such a manner? Both the visions of my future and my past are central to him. He is the key, but I do not know what he is the key *to*.

I roar out loudly in frustration as I enter the chaotic streets of Eltera. The townsfolk run around readying themselves for a fight, setting up barriers in the streets. Through the chaos I see Wistler and some of his men head into the guard tower just beyond the eastern gate. The ordinary citizens of Eltera continue taking up arms and setting up a ramshackle formation beyond the markets. Men and woman run back and forth carrying the swords, pikes, and shields that I have supplied from the armoury.

Storm clouds have begun to form darkened swathes above us, as if the gods are testing us. Without hesitation I make my way to the guard tower, my head pounding, my body aching like never before. Wistler's demise is the only thing keeping me going at this point.

A young girl knocks past me, her arms filled with bottles of spirits which I suspect will be paired with fire to create explosives. As I reach the base of the tower, I look upwards and see the narrow, stone staircase. My heart already races and my legs tremble from my adrenaline. There is so much that has happened in the last day, and my body grows weary. I will take great pleasure in stealing Wistler's life energy and watching him wither away.

I climb the steps at speed, imagining the different ways in which I can snuff out his life, the insolent pig.

When I reach the top, my foot catches the lip of the step and I stumble through the doorway. Not quite the intimidating entrance I was looking for.

Wistler awaits me, surrounded by six Wyverns. Two of them have taken up position and are pulling the chained mechanism to open the gate.

Wistler does not seem intimidated or surprised by my presence. In fact, his posture could not be more different from the bumbling oaf I have come to know since I landed in this kingdom. Before me stands a confident man, calm and in control. Seeing Wistler's face ignites a fierce rage within me, and it is all I can muster to stop my magic consuming me in my entirety.

"Wistler!" I roar. "Why? Why go through all this? You tried to have me assassinated!"

Wistler simply smiles, infuriating me further. He leans towards the embrasure in the wall, examining the happenings below. Then he brings his attention back to me.

"You have become quite the inconvenience, Lady Morgana, since your unplanned, unannounced arrival," he says through clenched teeth. Perhaps the frustration of the current situation is shared between us. "I had built something good. There was restlessness amongst the streets before the chaos of the witch trials. The taxations brought about by the king were taking effect, people were becoming harder to rule. I used the situation to build something good, something that made Eltera self-sufficient as a kingdom. More importantly, I kept the coin coming in."

"And this coin has not been shared with the crown. I imagine there is quite a large amount that could be used to help keep arms for King Athos and his armies," I answer. I have needed access to the forge for near two years now. This has caused a significant delay in my personal plans, not to mention the plans of the king.

"It is not my war that Athos continues to wage. He flexes his muscles in order to gain lands that Levanthria does not need, for resources that we do not need. He shows his power as a badge of honour, to make more people kneel, more people bow to him." Wistler laughs to himself. "Perhaps we are not too dissimilar after all."

"And the Barbaraqs? Why would you bring them to our shores?" Spit leaves my mouth as I curse the man in front of me. His Wyvern foot soldier stands primed, ready to attack me at any moment.

"How else am I going to take Askela? With the Barbaraqs by my side, people will have no option but to join the Wyverns. By the time the king returns – *if* he returns – he will be too late. Askela will have already fallen, and I will be declared ruler of these lands."

That is what all this is about. A power play for the crown by one of the lords of the lands. This is what happens when a king remains absent from his lands for so long. It is what I have warned Athos about persistently, to no avail. The king is as much to blame for this situation as Wistler. He has allowed Levanthria to become weakened to an attack, to allow the Barbaraqs to become confident enough to step foot on these lands once again.

Wistler looks out the window before a wry smile consumes his face, revealing his weasel-like features. "It looks like our friends are here." Two of the Wyverns continue pulling on the mechanism and drawing up the gates.

"There is only one problem, Wistler," I tell him. "I have already killed their chieftain. Who is it you expect to still have an agreement with?" Quietly, behind my back, I begin charging my hands with energy.

"Raegor has one daughter. It is her that will take his place, unless she is challenged by another in her ranks. From what I have heard, her savagery far exceeds others. She is renowned for her rage and her fury. If anything, you have poked the ant's nest in killing her father. I have no

doubts in my mind that she will want your head on a pike."
Wistler smiles. "I would go as far as saying that Yaelor was
often kept in line by her father. She prefers a more . . . *direct*
approach."

"At least I will get to have my fun with you first. You will
pay for your insolence." With that, I fire a blast of magic
towards the Wyverns standing before us. It connects with a
woman's face, and blood sprays across the room as she
drops to the ground where she violently convulses. Five
more to go. I want to leave Wistler for last so I can savour
ending his life.

Another Wyvern rushes forward and takes a wild swipe
at me, but they are clearly inexperienced; they would have
stood a better chance if they attacked me in numbers.
Although I can negate the effects of magic use through
channelling others, it still takes its toll on me. After all,
magic is not an endless stream I can dip into. It comes at a
price. Taking this into account, I remove a dagger from my
waist and ram it into my attacker's stomach. The man's skin
tears as my dagger buries deep within his gut, my hand
warming as his blood flows over my clenched fist. I stare
into his widened eyes and take note of their hazel colour
before twisting my blade violently. Bones and sinew crack as
I twist, and I pull the blade out before switching my gaze to
the remaining Wyverns. I will show them no mercy for
turning their back on their kingdom, on Levanthria.

I grow tired, but I know I must dig deep. Four of
Wistler's bodyguards remain. If I can get through the
remainder of this fight using minimal magic, I can reserve
my energy for the battle yet to come.

33

ORJAN

Rior and I make haste to the markets to gather with Eltera's defenders. From what I can tell, all the Wyverns are at the gates to greet the Barbaraqs with open arms.

When we arrive, I am surprised by the number of people who have volunteered to protect their homes, armed with all manner of weapons. We find Sparrow ready to lead the charge, clad in black leather armour that clings to her form. She grasps a sword in one hand and a round wooden shield in the other, which is decorated with the blue and white colours of Eltera. Heath stands beside her, having replaced one of his crutches with a pike and his torn tunic with chainmail. The crowd swells around them in restless anticipation.

It is a straight march from here to the city's gates.

"Orjan, you're here!" Sparrow seems somewhat reassured by my presence. "What happened to you?"

"Grush!" I rasp. Just mentioning his name brings my blood to a boil.

Sparrow's gaze drops to the blood-soaked shell in my hand, her eyebrows caving inwards. "You can fill me in later; we need to steady these people. They are scared. It has been centuries since Eltera defended itself from a siege and last time it was soldiers that stood on the front line, not street peddlers and barkeeps."

She is not wrong. The faces before me are awash with fear, yet those standing on the frontline wear expressions of rugged determination nonetheless.

"Those that can fight, move towards the front!" I call.

Nobody responds to me.

"Clear your ears out!" Heath bellows. "Orjan is here to fight beside you. This is not his kingdom, yet he stands here alongside you, ready to defend you and your families! Now set up formation as he asks!" Heath's impassioned words hammer into my heart.

"I know many of you will not trust me and I do not blame you," I say. "I have been lost for some time. But my path led me here, to this point." I move to stand next to Heath. "I have faced the Barbaraqs, and they fight with a blind viciousness that I have not seen before. They take what they wish, slaughtering anyone in their way. If we are to stand any chance, we need to hold our ranks, we need to stand firm, we need to stand together."

I peer down at Rior who stands by my side, taking in every word that I speak. "Morgana sends a messenger rides to Askela to call for support from their soldiers as we speak," I continue, making eye contact with the people in the crowd. "We need to hold off the Barbaraqs for as long as we can. If we do, we may just survive this day."

Heath raises his hand high into the air. "It is of this day that they will speak! They will tell of how the people of

Eltera stood up and fought, not only to defend our kingdom, but the whole of Levanthria!"

The crowd roars in tandem and as a group we fall into a better formation. I turn to face the street ahead of us, Sparrow on my left, Heath on my right.

"Do not break formation, we will use the streets to draw the Barbaraqs from the front. Keep the markets behind us and we will not face any surprise charges from the rear. Use your shields, and fight for one another!" I yell.

I feel a knock by my leg and realise that Rior is still firmly by my side.

"You are showing more bravery than I have ever seen from someone your age, Rior. You should take pride in your actions. If I were still a knight, I would have gladly trained you as a squire." I pat him on his head and ruffle his hair. In turn, he gives me a nervous smile.

We stare down the empty street in uncomfortable silence, waiting. Above, lightning flashes from the ever-darkening clouds. No sooner does the sky light up, a tremendous crash of thunder roars from above. Rain begins to fall down upon us, and I look up, embracing the cold rain falling onto my face.

Echoed cheers and war cries reach us from the eastern gates, Barbaraq drums hammering almost as loudly as the thunder that tries to crack open the skies. Nervousness sets in amongst the Elterian people, my own heart banging in tandem with the war drums. Barbaraq cheers bounce down the street towards us like stones skipping on water.

"Steady yourselves! They do this to illicit fear, to try and force us to break ranks. Hold your nerve and defend your brothers and sisters," I cry out as the noise coming from the oncoming Barbaraqs grows.

Then their fighters come into sight over the rise. They

charge, their axes, hatchets, and blades raised high as they scream towards us like a raging river. Their numbers far exceed our own.

"FOR ELTERA!" I roar.

"FOR LEVANTHRIA!" Health echoes.

Our people's own battle cries echo out and the noise is incredible. These people are untrained and unskilled in combat, but they make up for that with heart and passion.

I pull Rior behind me and brace myself with my shield as the first wave of leather-clad Barbaraqs crashes into us with tremendous force. I take no time to heave my shield forward, knocking back the first bare-chested warrior that reaches me. He tumbles to the muddy ground, and I am surprised at the speed at which Rior strikes out from behind me, plunging his knife into the Barbaraq like a viper. I heave my arm forward and slam my shield into the side of the head of another. Their jaw cracks from the force and blood sprays everywhere, soaking my face. I clench my fist tightly and aim a blow at his now misshapen face, sending him sprawling to the ground.

"Hold!" I know we need to stand firm against this initial push, and I plant my feet, bracing against the next Barbaraq who aims a swipe at me with his serrated sword. The weapon clunks heavily against my makeshift shield whilst Rior's dagger pokes out from underneath me, slashing against the Barbaraq's leg. The bald man grimaces but does not fall, instead taking another swipe at me. I embrace his blow before pushing back with force, slamming the bottom edge of my shield into his neck. Next, a woman comes at me bearing twin blades, moving with impressive speed.

"Step forward!" I scream, my throat burning as I give the command. I push into the woman and knock her backwards into her ranks. Our battle line steps forward, but we're not in sync. I remind myself that they have never done this before.

Elterian citizens step to either side of me, their wooden shields clattering into the wall of bodies in front of us. Then they follow with blows from their swords, taking down a row of Barbaraq warriors. Blood curdles with the mud underfoot, the heavy rain cascading a crimson river down the street. We continue to hold, withstanding wave after wave as bodies push against us, steel slamming against shields as the Barbaraqs frantically try to break us.

"Keep pushing back!" I shout over the cries of pain and anger. To my right, a few Elterians fall forward, leaving our formation exposed. The enemy seize their opportunity and pile into the gap, slicing through the fallen Elterians.

"Shit!" I curse as they push through our formation. "HOLD!"

But it is too late. Panic engulfs the front line and despite our best efforts, our formation begins to break at an alarming speed.

"Fall forward, push to the eastern gates!"

The only way we are going to survive now is to push through the Barbaraqs to the far side. I brace my shoulder behind my shield and charge forward. As bodies bounce off me, Rior and the fighters behind me take no time to dispatch the fallen in a brutal fashion. I continue to plough through anyone that is standing in my path and our fighters follow my tack. Bodies fall from both sides as cries of pain bellow out, mixed with the thunder and rain to fashion the most potent cocktail of chaos.

The numbers of our opponents begin to swell, and leather armour painted with the Wyvern colours flashes into my sight as a soldier brings an axe down upon me with both hands, bashing my shield. The force jolts me backwards and my heel catches against a body on the ground. The warrior slams his axe into my shield a second time and I tumble to the ground, landing on the bodies beneath me.

The smell of fresh blood overcomes me and limbs swing all around me as Barbaraqs and Wyverns clash against the Elterian people. My attacker seeks to finish me off, but they don't get chance; Sparrow rams through the crowd and plunges her sword deep into his stomach until it protrudes from his other side. She rips her sword back until it is free from the Barbaraq's flesh, his insides on full display as his blood splatters my face. Sparrow offers me a hand, hoisting me to my feet.

"Thank you."

"You can buy me a drink when all this is done," she answers, a wry smile on her face.

I parry an attack from behind. "I get the impression you are enjoying this."

Sparrow spins and extends her sword at an oncoming Wyvern, removing their head in a brutal yet elegant motion. "Why would I not embrace an opportunity to kill those that have oppressed us for so long?"

Another Wyvern moves towards her and it's time for me to return the favour. Drawing my arm back, I smash my shield into their chest, blasting them into the mud.

"There are too many of them!" I call out.

A brief opening appears through the battling parties, and within that space I see Grush dispatching two Elterians with a weapon I recognise: my morning star.

"GRUSH!" I call out, enraged. Any semblance of control is lost as my aggression consumes me more violently than any curse could.

He stands over a woman he has knocked to the ground

and our eyes meet. He smiles, then brings my morning star down on her with a sickening thud.

"NO!" The poor woman never stood a chance against such a brute.

I charge towards my enemy.

34

MORGANA

"Necromancy is the one magic class that should have remained forbidden. It draws on a darkness that should not be unleashed in this world. For this magic comes at great cost, in order to save the dead you need to offer a sacrifice. Some say you need to part with part of your soul."

Yuri Crier, Magic And Monsters Volume iV, 186KR

"KILL HER!" Wistler says through gritted teeth, pointing a finger in my direction. This time his Wyvern thugs move together and swing their weapons at me wildly. With one hand, I grab the sword of the man I have just killed and use it to block against the attack, desperately clutching my blood-soaked dagger in the other. I seize the opportunity and quickly swipe the smaller weapon against one of my attacker's necks. It cuts through his skin as though it is paper. He drops his weapon and clasps his hands tightly around his throat, but it is to no avail. Blood seeps between the gaps of his fingers as he collapses to the cold stone floor. Another swipe of a blade, this time from the only woman within this group. I duck her blow and step past her, drawing my sword across her front.

A hard boot to my side sends me hurtling into the wall and my shoulder cracks against it. Before I have time to think, there is a pressure pushing against my head, banging it off the stone. A flash of light fills my vision as I swear I see stars, and my head is yanked back as one of the Wyvern pulls me by my hair. He wraps his arm around my neck from behind, panting heavily as he seeks to garner control of me. Little does he know that not even the gods can control me.

"Fucking slut!" his words ring in my ear.

He spins me around to face Wistler as I pull down on his arm to create a small gap between it and my throat. Wistler is still smiling, despite me already killing four of his Wyverns.

"You are tenacious, Lady Morgana, I will give you that." He nods to the largest brute of the lot, who steps towards me with his sword outstretched. I kick my heel up into the balls of the man holding me, then bash my head back into his face. His grip loosens and I pull down on his arm again, darting to the side just in time as the other Wyvern plunges a sword into his stomach.

"Shit!" he curses as he draws the blade from his fellow enforcer's gut. Blood pools in the man's open mouth, spilling from his lip down his chest.

Seizing the opportunity, I cast a spell. "Septum, Spregu, Morta!"

The Wyvern holding the sword panics, then grunts in pain as I transfer his friend's fatal wound to him. The spell takes its toll on me, and I feel my fingers stiffen. Before the other Wyvern has time to think, I grab the arm of the Wyvern holding the sword and guide his arm back towards himself.

Not many men face the same death twice, but as I stab the sword through him, I smile. "Not bad for a slut!"

The two Wyverns collapse to the floor. When I turn to look for Wistler, there is no sign of him.

"Bastard!" I rush to the doorway and start descending the narrow stone steps, my vision still blurred from the blow to my head. The warmth of my blood streams down the side of my face, and a pain in my arm tells me I have been further wounded. My head grows drowsy, but I am determined to get to Wistler. He can't outrun me forever.

I misjudge a step and my foot slips. I am not able to react quickly enough, and before I know it, my vision is spinning wildly as I bounce down the steps, feeling each and every stone that my crumpling body crashes against. It is as though it takes an eternity to reach the bottom until finally, I slam against the wall and fall through the arched entrance.

My ears ring and I hear metal against metal, men and women screaming and roaring as Barbaraqs, Wyverns, and Elterians draw blood from one another. The ground is wet, a thick layer of mud forming which my hands sink into as I try to steady myself. They disappear in the thick muck, the rain lashing down against me, stinging my skin.

"Well, that's unfortunate."

I recognise Wistler's voice to my right, but before I have a chance to look, he kicks me in my side, sending me sprawling into the mud. Another heavy blow greets my head and I see stars once more as he strikes me again, then again.

I throw up an arm to strike him, but he is able to overpower me in my concussed state, landing another blow to my face. My nose and lip throb, the taste of iron seeping into my throat.

"Wistler," I gargle.

"You have made things harder than they needed to be with your arrival here. That ends now."

I feel a deep pressure in my stomach and my skin tears as he pushes a blade into my abdomen. A deep, agonising pain ignites inside the wound as I struggle to grip to my life. I have not seen this fate before. Perhaps the gods have had a change of heart, perhaps they have changed my destiny. Or perhaps they've been lying to me all this time.

"You will get in my way no more, Morgana." Wistler leans forward and offers me a patronising kiss on the cheek. He presses his sword deeper inside me and the pain extends beyond my back. Then he stands and takes his leave.

The sword remains protruding from my stomach as I face the darkened skies above. The rain stings my eyes and I start to accept my fate. The noise around me becomes a muffled distraction from my thoughts and as my breathing becomes laboured, I feel my pulsing heart-beat slow, each beat becoming more drawn out, making it hard to focus.

"No!" I force my eyes open. I will not let my life end in such a pointless manner. Dying in the mud in Eltera can't be how my fable ends. Taking a deep breath, I grab hold of the hilt of the sword and scream a guttural, animalistic cry as I pull it out. If I thought the pain was immeasurable as it pierced my skin, it is a thousand times worse removing it. I toss the blade to my side and clasp my hands over the wound. My blood pushes against my palms as I try in vain to stem the flow.

To my left, an Elterian fighter takes cover behind a horse cart that is tipped onto its side, and I know what I have to do. I will do what I must to survive this battle. This is not how the gods have foretold my future. I have bigger plans.

I stretch out my hand and unfurl my aching fingers. "Septum, Spregu –" I wince and take a deep breath, my pain unmanageable as my life slips away. "Septum, Spregu, Morta." I try to focus, my vision blackening. Nothing happens. I stretch out my fingers as best I can, desperate to make a connection with my forbidden magic. But it's too late. I'll die here in the mud, forgotten, a failure.

Then the man lets out an almighty shriek of pain and scrambles backwards into the cart, frantically pulling at his stomach as if something crawls underneath his skin. His clothing reddens as my fatal wound transfers to him. Confused panic engulfs his face, and as his breathing slows, his life draws to an end. A weight is taken from my chest, and suddenly I can breathe freely again. It is as though it is the first time I have taken in crisp, fresh air and I savour the sensation for a moment, I feel alive, I am alive. I roll onto my front and continue to breathe heavily. I have transferred one wound, but my others remain, and exhaustion keeps me from using any more magic.

Shrieking war cries come into focus and as I bring myself to my feet, the ensuing chaos of the battle is brought to the forefront of my attention. My dress is sodden, making it harder to move. Using the blade that Wistler nearly killed me with, I hack off the lower part of my dress. Foreign words call out near me, then again from another voice, then another. A word I do not understand is repeated by many of the Barbaraqs. Then I realise that their eyes are fixed on me as they call out to one another. They recognise me. They know it was I who killed their chieftain. I brace myself for the attack, exhausted and unsure how much longer I can endure.

Then the war cry of a woman catches my attention, and I realise the word that the Barbaraqs were shouting was a name.

Yaelor.

The slender-bodied, blood-soaked warrior bears down on me clutching hatchets in both her hands.

She wants revenge for what I did to her father.

35

ORJAN

Nothing but anger and rage consume me as I rush at Grush, who finally finishes clubbing a woman's head with my morning star. The distance between us shortens quickly as I bear down on the brute who stands in wait, unfazed by my intent to end his life. I use my shield to knock away anyone that gets in my way, the battle raging fiercely around me. As I clatter into him, he smashes my morning star against my shield. He falls from the collision, and in the process, I lose my own footing and slide face first through the thickening mud.

Nothing can prepare you for the sights of battle, the death that surrounds you. No one tells you about the smell, sweat and dirt tinged with a rusting stench. It is the latter that catches you off guard, provided by the sea of blood that has been shed.

The mixture of mud and blood washes over my face as I slide front first until eventually stopping. I heave myself to my feet as an enraged Grush is already charging at me. I raise my shield just in time as he crashes into me like a battering ram. My shield holds firm and I plant my feet in the mud, sliding backwards as he continues to push against me.

His snarling face is decorated with the blood of the fallen, and I am surprised his teeth do not crumble, such is the tightness of his jaw.

"Should have done this at the start!" he growls as a quick strike connects with my cheek. It is like his hand is made of stone, the force far stronger than I have known a man to possess. But then again, his hulking frame dwarfs everyone else on the battlefield.

"At last, something we agree on!" I throw my own fist at him, but Grush blocks this, pinning my arm under his own. I swing my shield from the other side, but he parries my attack and throws his boulder-like head into my face. A sharp, stinging pain sets in as my lip and nose begin to throb from the blow. Before I have time to think, he throws another headbutt at me, then another. Dazed, I stagger back as Grush then aims the morning star at me, and I jump back, barely avoiding the strike. Keeping his momentum, he spins and aims the weapon at me again. I raise my shield high to block him, the determination on Grush's face as clear as the intent of his actions.

He steps away from me for a moment, the two of us breathing heavily as we plan our next moves.

"When this battle is done, I am going to put your head on a spike for all to see. Anyone in this shithole will see how I played the dragon." Grush spits into the mud and raises his hands to offer me a turn to attack him.

"There is only one monster out of the two of us, and it isn't me!" I charge forward, my fists clenched tightly as I swing my shield and hammer it into Grush's side. He accepts the blow and although it no doubt causes him discomfort, it is only a blow capable of injury, not the death that I seek. Grush uses his arm to push my shield away, leaving my body open to an attack. He steps into my space and raises my morning star above his head.

Without a moment's hesitation, he brings it down against my arm holding the shield. With a crack, my arm falls limp, the spikes of the weapon piercing my tough skin. If not for the cursed body, I hold that blow would have likely taken my arm off.

My arm drops to my side, the weight of my shield dragging my shoulder down. The pain is harsh and unforgiving, and I know straight away that my arm is broken. I release an almighty roar, part in pain, part in anger, and Grush lunges forward with another boot to my chest, sending me hurtling back to the mud.

"See, that's where you belong, in the mud," Grush says. "No, you belong in the sewers, in fact!" He stands over me, the rain cascading down his face forming streaks of blood, some of it my own.

I heave as I breathe, my ribs aching, gasping for air. The way this thug fights is far beyond a simple enforcer. He has been trained. With brutal efficiency he has overpowered me even in my cursed state. His movement, however forceful, is skilled, each attack flowing into the next. I have never seen anything like it. I've underestimated him.

"Today, the dragon falls!" Grush raises his weapon above his head and brings it down on me.

With little other option, I grab hold of my shield with my good arm and drag it to my front, embracing the blow. The pain is like daggers tearing though my skin and muscle as my bones crunch under the force, a knot of pain in my stomach clenching tightly like a giants fist. But it works. The power pushes my broken arm into my front, and I scream out in agony as Grush throws down blow after blow against it. Each time it is as if a headed blade pushes through my skin, and with each strike I wonder if it will be the last. I grit my teeth and dig as deep as I can. Deeper than the treacherous waters of Yugo's Tears. If I can survive that, I can survive this. Each time he strikes me, a painful memory flashes into my mind as clear as if I am in the moment.

The burning village, the drink I consumed as I found myself exiled from Rashouya, the gambling it led to. Vireo beating me in the street, the painful moment I told Laith that he could no longer be my squire for I had no chance of regaining the honour I had lost.

The pain travels up to my shoulder and across my chest as Grush continues to rain down blows against my shield. He could easily end this fight, but he knows what he is doing. He wants me to experience this pain, he wants to prolong it.

Flashes of Zerina allowing me on her ship, then a card game where Esara reveals to me her glamour magic, followed by a ship in flames as it sinks to the depths of the ocean. One by one, blow by blow, these memories bay through my mind, each and every act and consequence that led to me being here in this moment splayed out in the mud as my life is about to end. As the memories shred through my thoughts, my fight wavers and my instincts fade, as does my will to live. I deserve this fate, I deserve everything that has happened to me, for the lives I have impacted, for those that have been lost because of the decisions I made. My envoy, Ulrik, Bravor, Preya. They would all be alive on this day if not for me, along with many others.

I can't hold on any longer, and my shield and arm fall to my sides. I can't take the pain. Above me, a fork of lightning darts in between the blackened clouds. Rain lashes against my face as I wallow on my back, my body and spirit broken.

It is all I can ask to let the gods end the misery I have endured for a lifetime.

"Look at you, you really are pathetic, Dragon. I expected more!" Grush stares down and for a moment I see pity in his eyes. He raises my morning star high above his head for a final time and I close my eyes, accepting my fate.

Grush cries out. I open my eyes and see Rior standing beside him, the dagger I gave him embedded in Grush's leg.

"Leave him alone!" Rior screams.

Infuriated, Grush swings the back of his hand against Rior's face, sending him rolling through the mud. "You little shit!" he growls. He grabs the hilt of the dagger and grimaces as he pulls it from his leg. "I should have killed you whilst you sat with your fallen keeper."

Grush limps towards Rior who shows rugged determination and courage as he drags himself back to his feet, raising both his fists towards Grush, staring him down through his blackened eyes.

"You know they say there is a special place in the afterlife, especially for those who show cowardice and take their own life. Think of the things the demons down there will be doing to your keeper right now," Grush taunts.

"I – I'm not afraid of you," Rior says.

"Oh, but you should be." He aims a fatal blow at the boy.

"Rior!" I can't see the boy die. I told him to stay by my side, I vowed to free him, I vowed to defend him. I heave myself to my feet, using more strength than I have to fight the urge to give up. Then I throw myself weakly at Grush and grab hold of his arm, stopping his strike.

His arm is taut with tension as he struggles against me. I have enough strength in my good arm to match him, fueled by my desire to protect the boy.

"There will be an even worse place in the afterlife for

you!" I roar, and for the first time, it is fear that flickers across Grush's face. A primal urge takes over me and I do something I have never done: I bite down on Grush's arm. A metallic taste seeps into my mouth as my pointed teeth tear through his flesh with ease. Grush screams out in agony and drops my morning star. I don't stop until my teeth meet his bone. He pulls his arm away from me and as he does, his flesh leaves his arm, clinging to my chin.

I stare into his dark eyes, and I swear to the gods in this moment I see right through to his soul. He steps back away from me but my rage controls me now. The things he has done, the torture he has inflicted on behalf of the Wyverns; the man is a scourge on these lands, one I intend to free this kingdom from. I endure the pain as I pry my arm free from the shield and toss it to Rior. The boy scurries towards it and picks it up with both hands to cover himself.

As I step forward, my foot kicks against my morning star. Spitting out Grush's bloodied flesh, I pluck my old weapon from the mud, then bring my eyes level with him once more.

Grush looks around him as he searches for something to defend himself with. Seeing a pike skewed into a Wyvern body nearby, he races towards it. I chase after him, every inch of my body aching, my legs burning as I force myself across the bloodied, body-laden terrain. A Barbaraq gets in my way but I hammer their chest with my morning star, causing them to crumple to the ground, their chest ripped open in an instant. Grush reaches the pike and growls as he grabs hold of it with both hands, pulling it from the Wyvern corpse. Then he turns to face me.

It is clear from his widened eyes that he is surprised by the speed with which I move, and I am already upon him. I roll into the side of the pike with my broken arm to knock it sideways, leaving Grush's body open. Then I spin towards him, my morning star outstretched, every painful memory at the forefront of my mind as I let out an almighty scream. With a sickening squelch, the head of my morning star connects with the side of Grush's head. His blood sprays everywhere as he collapses to the ground. I stand over him, watching his body twitch whilst blood pools around his head.

"This is the day Eltera will remember that it was the dragon who freed them from the monster!" Without a moment's hesitation, I bring my morning star down onto his head once more, then again and again, leaving nothing but a pool of pulp

36

MORGANA

Bodies from both sides pile everywhere, but the Elterians are losing the fight and their numbers are slowly dwindling as the Barbaraqs continue with their onslaught. The storm cracks and boils above us as fierce and unforgiving as the battle itself.

Yaelor races towards me with a hatchet clasped in each of her hands, her face etched with anger. Her hair is tied back into tight plaits, and half of her face is painted blue. The other half is painted with her hatred towards me.

She takes a frenzied swing at me with a hatchet, and when I dodge this, she follows up with a swing of her second weapon. I barely evade the full force of the blow, and the sharpened edge of the weapon slices through my dress, stinging my skin as it cuts into me. I fire a blast of energy at her, but I miss Yaelor and my spell connects with a Wyvern behind her. Using the magic causes my hand to crack and I wince in pain. I have used a considerable amount of magic on this day and even though I can channel these spells through other people's life force, even I know that I have my limits. The gods will only allow me to consume so much.

Yaelor is quickly upon me and lands a blow to my face, snapping my head back. She swings her hatchets at me again, but I duck underneath, grabbing at a bloodied sword on the ground. Though the Barbaraqs are known for their unrefined fighting style, this woman is a skilled warrior. She takes another swing at me, cutting through the back of my dress. This time the cut bores deeper into my shoulder and I am lucky to be alive. Had she been a little bit closer, she would have likely killed me. Spinning towards her, I hold my sword outstretched, parrying her next strikes.

"You are not just a shaman, you can fight," Yaelor tells me, almost as if she approves. Though her words are broken and fragmented, I am surprised to learn that she speaks our tongue so well. She brings down both hatchets upon me and I raise my sword to block them. Our weapons connect, and we press against one another, staring into one another's eyes. Her toned muscles flex with the effort, her skin shimmering in the rain. I stare deep into her emerald-green eyes that are marbled with blue. Dark freckles decorate her nose and cheeks. A stab of recognition rips through me.

It can't be. Not after all this time. Why would the gods toy with me in such a cruel way?

"Ferelda?" I stammer, shocked.

Yaelor stops instantly and steps back from me, resting her weapons by her side. "Where did you hear this name?"

"Ferelda, is it really you?" I ask, desperation coming over me.

"How do you know this name!" Recovering from the distraction, she sends me a warning blow, which I quickly parry.

"It is you!" I breathe. "It's me, Queren." It is a name I have not spoken for a long time, one that I banished with my dark memories as I became someone new. "It is I, your sister."

Yaelor looks dumbfounded, her eyes darting from side to side as she searches through her own memories.

I grab hold of the pendant around my neck and raise it. "This, this is the pendant you made for me with Mother. I have never removed it." I watch as Ferelda eyes me with distrust. I do not blame her. "How – how are you here, how are you with the Barbaraqs?" I continue. "I thought you were dead." I have so many questions, but the battle continues to unfold furiously around us.

She frowns. "Raegor raised me, taught me how to fight." It is as though Yaelor battles with her own thoughts. She was taken by the Barbaraqs as a child after they burnt our village to the ground. She was only a young girl then, and I panic, realising that she might not even remember.

I drop my sword to the floor and slowly edge towards her. "You were stolen from me, Ferelda. They destroyed our home, killed our father."

Yaelor drops her weapons to the ground and raises her hand towards my face. She rests her fingers against my cheek, and my eyes swell with tears. I raise my own hand and place it against her own blood-soaked face. Her cheek is warm and the rain cascades down on us as we take each other in.

My sister is alive. I care of nothing else.

I begin to sob into her hand, not from heartbreak or grief but from relief. It is as though the darkest of clouds that has burdened me all of my life is suddenly lifted, replaced by the clearest of skies. The things I have done, the path that I have walked, the things that have happened to me. The fate that I have accepted as I believed my sister to be dead. I sought to avenge her memory and now she stands before me very much alive.

I take my hand from her face and place it over hers which still remains on my cheek. Her skin is rough. She has a warrior's hands, but in this moment, her hand trembles.

"I love you," I tell her. They are the only words that I can muster.

She pulls her hand away from mine and steps away from me, looking around at the death that surrounds us.

"*Kurri, kurri*!" she yells out and the other Barbaraqs begin to shout the word in turn.

Panicked, I take in the scene before me as her people rally to her cries.

"I am sorry, Queren." She picks up her hatchets from the mud. With one last glance at me, she begins to run towards the eastern gates. The Barbaraqs follow.

"Ferelda!" I call out in hope that she will turn back around, that she will remain here with me. But she doesn't.

As quickly as she re-entered my world, my baby sister is gone, like the passing storm above.

Dumbfounded, I stand staring through the gates as the Barbaraqs fall back and leave. The remaining Wyverns stand in total confusion, weapons still clutched firmly in hand. The Elterians gather with renewed determination as they start to push back against our enemy.

Out of the corner of my eye, a flash of purple catches my attention. There is only one person in this kingdom pompous enough to sneak past a battlefield in vibrant silks.

I made a promise to that man, and I intend to keep it.

"Wistler!" My voice reigns over the battlefield.

Wistler seeks to weasel his way towards the eastern gate in pursuit of the Barbaraqs, showing every ounce of his cowardice.

My body is exhausted, and I know I will bear the consequences of using my magic, but the temptation is too much. I throw my hand forward and channel the ancient power that courses through my body. A blackened force of energy presses Wistler into the outer wall of the city and freezes him in place.

"Morgana, stop! Stop this!" Wistler squirms as I force him up into the air so everyone can see what I am about to do.

My body strains with effort, and small indentations begin to form on my outstretched hand as if something squeezes it tightly, compressing my bones. I fight through the pain and remain focused on Wistler.

A loud crack is followed by a shriek as I slowly and painfully begin to crush and break every one of his bones, starting at his ankles and working my way up. Wistler howls in pain, screaming, begging for it to stop.

"You deserve every second of this pain and torment," I tell him as his arms break, leaving bones protruding as blood splashes in the mud underneath him. His chest begins to crack and heave, his eyes bulging out of their sockets. The fighting stops as all turn to watch Wistler's torture, his shrill screams echoing for all to hear. His whimpers become childlike as the crushing of his bones reaches his neck. Blood seeps from every orifice.

"P – please," he rasps, shaking violently.

With a flick of my hand his neck snaps. I release my hold and he crumples in a heap on the ground below. My connection to my magic feels weak, as if it might snap at any moment like a frayed rope. I have never pushed myself this far before. Fire and ice flow through my skin and I let out my own scream of pain and anguish. I drop to my knees as my body fights the affliction. Even using the small amount

of magic required to absorb another's life force would risk
tipping me too far. My mind would break.

As I grit my teeth and force myself to my feet, I notice
that the battle has stopped, everyone around me stares in
disbelief. Across the street towards the market, I see Orjan
standing tall, his right arm hanging limply from a drooped
shoulder. In his other hand, he grasps a blood-soaked
weapon. One by one, the Wyverns begin to drop their
weapons and raise their hands in surrender.

Orjan lifts his weapon into the air and begins to roar.
Others follow him, hoisting their weapons as they cheer in
celebration.

Many have fallen but the battle for Eltera is over. The
people of this kingdom, led by Orjan, have won.

.

37

ORJAN

Elven blood is only distinguishable by its bitter metallic taste, even then only seasoned alchemists would be able to spot the traces of Elven heritage. Such is the level of dilution this once great bloodline faces.
    Loran Elora, Scriptures of Elves Volume III, 87KR

THE DARKENED sky above passes with the storm, allowing light to fall on Eltera. Many people have fallen on this day from all sides on what has been the bloodiest day in Eltera's history. But it's over.

As my adrenaline subsides, my broken arm causes me considerable discomfort, my drooping shoulder making me slump to one side.

"This will sting." A young man tends to Rior who sits in the back of a cart by the tavern. There are many lined up side by side as the people set about tending to the wounded and moving the bodies to a place of rest.

Rior winces as the healer places a damp cloth against his eye to wash away the blood and dirt that cling to him. The boy's eye is swollen shut, the purple swelling flowing into his enlarged cheek and down to his bloodied mouth. He doesn't say a word. It is as though he stares into a void beyond the healer.

"You showed great bravery today, Rior," I tell him gently. It is unlike anything I have seen from a child his age. He would have been forgiven for running from the battle and hiding, freezing when blood started to be shed. Instead, he stood and fought alongside the other people of this kingdom.

"I owe you my life. If not for your intervention, I am sure that I would not be standing here now." I place my hand on the boy's shoulder and squeeze gently to show my thanks. "You have shown great bravery," I tell him, "but you will need time." At such a young age I know that the atrocities he has seen on this day will haunt him for some time. He is going to need help with this, he is going to need support. "I am here for you, Rior. I will help you through whatever it is that is to come."

Rior doesn't move or look at me.

"Besides, I am in need of a squire," I add. I am no longer a knight, but I can still train the boy. Not since Laith have I taken a squire. It is time that I moved on.

"A squire?" Rior's face brightens as a swelled smile forms in the corner of his mouth.

"*After* you have recovered," I say, smiling. Then I hesitate for a moment. "I am proud of you, Rior." A lump forms in my throat. "You have my honour and my sword."

Rior blushes and averts his gaze, hiding a happy smile.

I take in the blood-stained streets of the surrounding markets. People mourn the fallen but they go about their day. Though they are now liberated from Breyton's tyranny, it will take time to recover. The brutality that Morgana showed Breyton in his final moments was like nothing I have ever seen. Dark magic broke him apart as his final moments were spent in agony. It is exactly what he deserved, but the power Morgana holds is something I wish never to fall foul of. I know not which gods are on her side but the power she wields dwarfs anything I have seen in these lands or beyond.

"Orjan." Morgana's voice startles me. She stands before me as broken as I am, her blood-streaked clothes torn and bathed in mud. I can see gashes against her skin through the tears in her dress, which appears to have been hacked off. Her hair clings to her face and her puffed up eyes combined with the streaks running through her dirtied face tell me she has shed tears recently. It shocks me. I have only known Morgana to be cold, calculated, and determined, every action carefully planned to achieve whatever outcome she desires. She did not need to fight in the streets with these people, but for some reason, she did.

"Morgana." I bow my head to her.

"I wanted to thank you for all that you have done," she says. "You have played your part in defeating the Wyverns."

"It is no less than they deserved," I say. "What of those that remain?"

Morgana smiles. "There are too many for the dungeons. Many gave up arms as soon as they saw their leader dead. My concern is that they could rise up again. This is why I have come to speak to you. I have another task to ask of you."

Given the conditions of which this task was set, I feel as though I have little option other than to follow exactly as the sorceress commands. "What is it you ask?"

"I cannot stay here," she starts. "I have an urgent matter that I need to resolve. On the far side of Eltera sits a forge, known for its magical properties. It is key in the production of ironite armour."

I have heard of this metal before. Its hardened compounds make it one of the strongest armours that can be forged. I had no idea that it sat here.

"It is why I am here. My research found that it is here where it lies, hidden and dormant. I think I have found the key to unlocking its power. It will take research and time, but I feel we will be able to turn the tides on the King's War."

"And what part do I play in this?" I ask.

"Wistler governed this kingdom. As you have seen, he is no more. I need someone here who can bring stability to these people. Someone who they will follow and listen to. I also need someone who can lead these Wyverns and keep them in check, that will stop them from taking over again. I want you, Orjan. I want you to be that person."

I am taken aback by her words. "You want me to govern Eltera?

"This is what I ask."

The magnitude of what she asks of me is far greater than I could ever have expected. "If that is what you wish of me, then so be it."

"Take my warning though, Orjan. Governing comes with great difficulty. Know that despite your best efforts, there will always be people that suffer, that your decisions will always have consequence."

"All I ask is that these people do not endure the hardships that they have faced recently." I cast my eyes over Rior.

"There is more. As reward for your word, I will uphold my promise that I will do what I can to try and rid you of your curse." Morgana reaches her hand slowly to my face and grimaces momentarily as I feel the weight of my skin become lighter. My jaw moves freely and I show her my uncursed smile. Her eyes widen at the sight of my true face, and for a moment, it is as if we are the only ones here in the street. Then she lets out a grunt of pain before letting go, her legs almost giving way as I return to my cursed form.

"It is a powerful magic that binds you to this curse. I will do what I can to try and free you from it, although I do not know how long it will take me or even if I can free you of its bindings."

For the first time I feel as though there is a way to return to my former self, and it gives me something I did not think possible: hope.

"I will do what I can, as best I can," I tell her.

"Well, it is settled then." Morgana turns to face the gathering crowd. "Let it be known that Orjan now governs Eltera in place of Lord Wistler." She pauses for a moment. "And in place of Breyton." She turns to point at me. "This man has helped liberate this fallen kingdom and I ask this of him on behalf of the absent King Athos."

There is a silence beyond the ground as they absorb what Morgana tells them, and I move to stand beside her as she addresses them. Rior looks up at me and smiles. In this moment, I know I have his blessing.

Chanting starts ringing out from the people. A word I have come to hate as it was used to belittle me, to humiliate me. They bring a new meaning to it now as they cheer. They say it as a compliment, as an honour. I will own this word, this title.

But it will also be a warning to anyone who seeks to bring despair to the walls of this city again.

"Dragon, Dragon, Dragon!"

The crowd's cheers echo loudly for all across Levanthria to hear.

38

MORGANA

J onah has finally succumbed to my ways, his body too
fragile, his mind too weak. I knew he was withholding
information from me. Now I am hopeful that with the
forge I will be able to unlock the magical properties
within ironite. With this I will be able to imbue armour and
weapons with magic, if my theories are correct that is.

Diary entry of Morgana, 255KR

IT HAS TAKEN a whole day of rest for me to be able to speak
with anyone at the castle. I take solace in knowing that
Orjan will be here to govern Eltera. He will do better than
Wistler ever managed. I will see to it that that coward's name
is removed from the history books. No one will speak his
name, no one will know he existed. His family line falls with
him, and it is no less than he deserves.

I make my way to the courtyard, my mind set on my next
task. Before I do anything else, I need to find my sister, I
cannot leave things how they are. If I need to leave Levanthria to find her then I will.

"Have the workers begin transporting that forge to Askela, I will not risk losing access to it again." I can ensure that production of armour is produced which will please the king. Even more so if my theories of what can be achieved with this forge prove true. This will surely bring me favour with the king and enhance my chances of him taking me as his queen. True, it will take some time to transport it, but it will be worth it in the end. I refuse to spend another day in this kingdom. It has already cost me more time than I care. On the other side, I feel as though the gods are slowly playing their hands with their twist of fate, showing me that my sister is alive, someone who I had long accepted as being dead.

With Orjan watching over Eltera – and as long as I can keep him close to me and preferably on side – I will be able to cheat my death. Laith will have no need to avenge Orjan if he is alive and prospering.

As I move through Eltera on horseback, the city gates open, allowing entry of a convoy of soldiers who enter at a gallop. It is a welcome face that I see as the group approaches me.

"Codrin!" His stony Elven face is a welcome sight. "I am just about to leave, but I will update you on who now runs this kingdom. We need to get our spell casters here to begin researching the forge straight away."

Codrin doesn't acknowledge my words as he pulls up next to me on his horse. He has become quite the obedient dog as he has followed the kings and my direction in Askela since Jareb fell. His Elven features are accentuated by the sun shining behind him as if he has been sent by the gods to collect me.

His face is adorned by grief, an emotion I have never

seen from this man before. Up until now I would have sworn the elf was unable to show any form of emotion.

"Lady Morgana, I bring word from the war."

"What is it?" I ask, frowning. I have had no visions, seen no omens. Whatever it is that Codrin wishes to tell me, it is something the gods have not allowed me to see.

"King Athos is dead."

OTHER BOOKS IN THE LEVANTHRIA SERIES

A Forest Of Vanity And Valour

A Sea Of Sorrow And Scorn

A Frost Of Fear And Fortitude

A Loch Of Grace And Greed - Free Short Story

Dust - Free Short Story

Coming Soon And Available For Pre-Order

A Stone Of Destiny And Despair

A House Of Powder And Plot

A Frost Of Death And Deceit

A Forest Of Bastards And Betrayal

JOIN MY NEWSLETTER

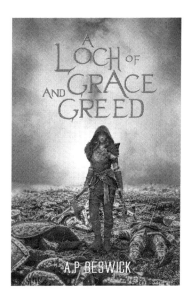

I hope you enjoyed this story. If you would like to keep up to date with my books as well as read one of my free short stories you can do so HERE

Made in the USA
Monee, IL
04 April 2024

56376967R00142